CW00969153

JILL TRESEDER was born in
childhood in sight of the sea
Cornwall and West Wales. She
Devon overlooking the River D

After graduating from Bristol with a degree in German,
Jill followed careers in social work, management development
and social research, obtaining a PhD from the School of
Management at the University of Bath along the way.

Since 2006 she has focused on writing fiction.

ALSO BY JILL TRESEDER

PRAISE FOR HER NOVELS

For *Becoming Fran*
'What seems to be a lovingly observed tale of growing up in provincial England in the 1960s turns out to be something much more, with a satisfying plot that creeps up on you unawares with an intriguing slow-burn complexity.'
Mark McCrum

For *The Hatmaker's Secret*
'A beautifully written, intriguing and touching story of the effects of racial prejudice across generations. A compelling and satisfying read.'
Judith Allnatt

For *The Saturday Letters*
'This is a deep and powerful story which has its origins during the time of slavery… Jill Treseder has created a wonderful character full of depth and also sadness. She is rich and engaging and her language is simply wonderful, really adding authenticity to her story. A fabulous novella…full of substance.'
JB Johnston

For *My Sister, Myself*
Beautifully engaging…an emotive and captivating story about the troubled lives of two sisters divided by the experiences they

THE
Birthday
HOUSE

JILL TRESEDER

Helen

best wishes

Jill T—— ——.

June 2019.

SilverWood

Published in 2019 by SilverWood Books

SilverWood Books Ltd
14 Small Street, Bristol, BS1 1DE, United Kingdom
www.silverwoodbooks.co.uk

ISBN 978-1-78132-879-8 (paperback)
ISBN 978-1-78132-888-0 (ebook)

British Library Cataloguing in Publication Data
A CIP catalogue record for this book is available from the British Library

Page design and typesetting by SilverWood Books
Printed on responsibly sourced paper

In memory
of
Chris and Army

Acknowledgements

I would like to thank Keith Poole for his knowledge of the history and products of Dartmouth Pottery; Richard Webb for memories of his friendship with Chris and her family; and Martin Thomas at www.dartmouth.photos for the cover image.

Susan 2018

I sometimes wonder what would have happened if my best friend hadn't been murdered by her father when we were both twelve years old. What difference might it have made to my life?

I might be one of those people who go to school reunions to celebrate fifty or sixty years of friendship with prosecco and canapés. Josephine Kennedy. I wonder what she would look like now? Much the same, is my guess. Would she have married? I could have spent hours swapping stories with her, instead of marking that grim anniversary every year by drinking half a bottle of single malt and waking up, shivering, beside the cold ashes of a dead fire. A vigil of a kind, I suppose.

Jo's father also killed her mother and their dog, of course, not to mention himself. But, much as I liked her mother and loved that old mongrel, she would probably be dead by now, and Rusty certainly would, so that hasn't really affected me. Not in a practical way, that is. But it did affect me in processing the event. It was such a large *quantity* of death to come to terms with.

What other differences might it have made?

I would be able to drive up the hill past her old house with its pretty windows and it wouldn't be in the least bit spooky, just happily nostalgic. Jo might come and stay with me, and we'd do that together, reminiscing about the games we used to play, having a good laugh.

I might have trusted a man long enough to get married; or even have lived a while with a man, sharing a bed and cooking together; or at least have been in what people would call a "relationship" that lasted more than six months.

I might be a woman who could cry.

I might be a person who could forget to lock the door at night, instead of having so many locks, bolts and alarms that it takes fully ten minutes to put them all in place. Not that any amount of security of that kind would have made a jot of difference to Jo's fate. Any pop psychologist would be quick to see the metaphor in all this. I'm well aware that the bogeyman I'm guarding against is my own emotions. They got shut down all those years ago and I'm happy to keep them that way. It's how I am.

Then there's that other question. What if people back then – my parents, that is – had told me the truth about what happened? What difference might *that* have made?

I might have many more friends than I do. For I might have continued to approach life in the spirit of trust and risk-taking that led to my friendship with Jo. I might not always have been so guarded, so suspicious of the stories people told me, for fear that they were hiding some secret and making a fool of me.

At a deeper level, though, that second question has considerable significance. Concealing the truth from a child is robbery, in my view. The right to be in direct control of my life was stolen from me. My parents imposed a filter between me and events. I was dependent on an interpreter – in isolation, quarantined from life, immune system compromised. Of course, they meant well, my parents. The most universal excuse. The most damning indictment.

Not that I'm unhappy with my life. I broke free from all that, albeit at great cost to family relationships. I've been successful and respected in my field; although in other circumstances I doubt I would have chosen the police force. I was a dreamer as a child and had fantasies of becoming a painter. But I was pushed into science by parents and teachers, and that shaped my career. I've dabbled in watercolours as a relaxation over the years and people have urged me to take up painting in retirement. But it's too late now. Suppose I discovered I had a great talent? How would I come to terms with all those wasted years?

Be that as it may, the police in general and forensics in particular, seemed a logical choice at the time – to work in an environment where it was reasonable to question what people told me; where I would have to face harsh realities head-on; where I would have the opportunity to study the criminal mind. All at one remove, of course. No direct contact – at least, not with the living. For me, it was enough to be operating within an organisation that represented law and order.

Which brings me to the only truly significant question: why did Jo's father act as he did? Forget the idle speculation of these somewhat self-indulgent "What-if?" enquiries. The event has always obsessed me. I have revisited it several times over the years to uncover what happened and how. The mystery of why he did it remains. It is now the only question I'm interested in addressing.

1954–5

Mrs Harrison, Housekeeper

It's crisp when I set off. But sunny. I like these mornings with leaves all brassy against the blue sky like a kiddie's painting. I like the walk, looking across the river. As my Bert likes to say, "God's in his heaven – all's right with the world!" There's *Similarity* alongside the wharf, over at Kingswear – such a pretty colour for a dirty job. Whoever thought of painting a whole fleet of coaling ships primrose yellow? My Bert's always asking me why I come all the way out here, when I could get plenty of work right in the middle of Dartmouth. But I like Mrs Kennedy. She's a gentle soul, and we have a nice chat over a cup of tea. Horniman's, yellow label, she has. Not Typhoo like us. And a biscuit to go with it, Rich Tea or a ginger nut.

Here's the creek. I always think Warfleet looks kind of mysterious, what with the water always being that dark green. There's the old brewery – fancy pottery they make there now. I often wonder if Mr K's watching me from his office as I walk past. But why would he? He's a busy man, Mr Harold Kennedy. A difficult boss, though. My friend knows his secretary. *Ex*-secretary, that is. She gave notice, she was that fed up with his moods, and got a position up at the Naval College. He's very particular, she said. Which is good, and she coped with that, but the tempers and storming about was too much. Then next day, it would all be forgotten and he'd be all smiles and charming again. Not an easy husband, either, reading between the lines of my tea and chat with Mrs K. But he dotes on the daughter. Sweet girl, Josephine, always very polite.

Lovely dahlias up there. What a show. Mind you, I don't like the earwigs you get in them. But they're all right, just so long as you don't bring them in the house. Nearly all the trees are turning. Winter's not far off, but there's still a lot of heat in that sun. Especially going uphill.

My friend says there's a rumour going round. Mrs K's been seen. Getting into a car, getting out of a car. Tongues will wag. I've been wondering if I should say anything to her. Warn her, like. But you can never be sure. She might be upset with me. Wouldn't want to lose me job, when there might be no truth in it. I don't approve of that sort of thing, but you could hardly blame her, with Mr K being so difficult. Probably best to keep my mouth shut. Keep out of other people's business, that's what my Bert always says.

This hill gets steeper every time I come. I'll walk on the shady side. Wonder what she'll want me to do today. Bedrooms and change the sheets, I shouldn't wonder. On the way home I'll get us a nice bit of fish for tea. Bert likes a bit of fish. Spot of parsley sauce, mashed potatoes and finish up those carrots. There's Mrs Always-Gardening giving me a wave. That's what Mrs K calls her neighbour, so I just think of her as Mrs A-G.

I push on up the hill. Nearly there. There's a couple of rooks hopping from fence post to fence post, keeping just ahead of me. Like a couple of old men. They make me laugh out loud. At that, they take off and settle on the roof of the Kennedys' house, prancing along the ridge tiles. It's as if they're leading the way. People are always saying, what pretty windows – and that's true – but they don't think of one thing. They're a pain in the neck to keep clean.

I cross the road, out of the shadow into the sun, up their path. Oh, that's funny. He hasn't taken his *Times*. So I suppose he's home. Oh dear. I'd better take it up to the house. Good idea of his, putting that piece of drainpipe there. Keeps the paper dry and saves the paperboy going up the drive. Better not go in the front in case he's about. Those Michaelmas daisies are a picture.

Ouf! This back door's always so stiff. Oh my! Washing-up not done. That's not like her. Maybe she's ill. No sign of anybody. Ah well, I'll clear up here and then she'll be down, like as not, to tell me what she wants doing. Coat and bag on hook. Where's me apron?

The house is so quiet, it gives me the shivers. And no Rusty. Odd. He usually rushes to greet me. Nearly knocked me over when he was younger. Now, just don't start imagining things. They must be sleeping in. Up all night with a tummy bug. Something like that, I'll be bound. And Rusty will be on Josephine's bed, that's for sure. That's better. Nothing like a bowl of hot soapy water. I'll have this cleaned up in no time.

There goes the phone in the living room. She'll answer it from upstairs. They've got one by the bed. Oh blow! It's going on. Oh dear, maybe I should pick it up. But I don't like them things. Never know what to say. Where's that towel? Dry me hands. Oh, curtains still drawn. Lights left on. And the electric fire, extravagant people. There it is over by the window. Dusted it often enough.

'Yes…? No. She's not here. I'll go and…'

I turn round to see if she might be coming in to rescue me in that nice green housecoat of hers that goes so well with her

19

coppery hair. And then I see it. Him. It.

I turn back quickly, focus on a fly that's walking up the windowpane.

'Please phone 999 for me,' I hear myself say. 'Call the police. Get an ambulance here. Something terrible…' I put the receiver down and make for the door, careful to face the wall. Can't stay in here a moment longer. I feel all arms and legs, telling my feet where to go. And what about her? Mrs K? I must see to her. I start up the stairs. Halfway up I can see the bedroom door. Closed. I stop dead. I listen. The silence is hard and heavy. Like I could catch hold of it. It's as if there's a gate across the stairs, like the one Bert made when the kiddies were small. I can't pass the gate. I dare not open that bedroom door. It's as if a black mist rolls down the stairs on top of me.

Then there's a terrible noise, which is me screaming and running back down into the kitchen and out the door and stopping to retch and retch in the flowerbed, poor Michaelmas daisies, and on down the path and skidding on the gravel so fast I have to grab the cherry tree trunk at the gate to stop landing in the road, and along the footpath and across the road and down the neighbour's drive, longer than I thought, and yelling, 'Help! Help!' to find Mrs A-G, and she's holding me up and dragging me inside to sit me down, and her husband looms with a glass and tells me to drink and it catches my breath and burns down into me. And I'm saying to them, '999. Phone 999,' although that's already been done. And he's given me his big handkerchief and I breathe in the smell of fresh ironing and pipe tobacco, which is comforting.

I can hear his voice in the hall, clipped and precise, and I think, yes, you can imagine him in charge of an aircraft carrier, which I think he was. And then he's back and asking me, 'Burglary, was it? Have they been broken into?'

And I start to say, 'It's…' but I can't go on and have to press the handkerchief against my mouth in case I have to vomit again.

I can feel them exchanging glances above my head and then we all hear the siren coming nearer, and he says he'd better go next door and meet the police, and I say, 'Don't look…' but again I can't go on and I clutch the handkerchief and stare at the blue light flashing and reflecting off the silver jug on the windowsill to blot out the image that's spattered over the inside of my brain.

And Mrs A-G is rocking me and saying, 'Don't upset yourself,' but it wasn't me that upset myself, and then she says, 'It'll all be all right,' but it won't be all right and nothing will ever be all right ever again.

She holds out the glass again, but I shake my head.

I push up out of the chair. 'I don't know what came over me. I must be getting back. Meet the police. It's the least I can do.' I have an obligation. I can't be leaving them to strangers coming in the house.

Mrs A-G tries to hold me back, but I tell her I'll be fine and I make my legs walk straight to show her.

'Anyway, I have to fetch my coat and my bag's still in the kitchen,' I say as if that's the most important thing in the world.

The sergeant asks me questions and then Mr A-G takes me home in his motor. They've got Bert home from work and I'm glad he's a man who can make a pot of tea. Bert sits across from me and he says I have to put it out of my head. But it's all lodged in there like it's part of the furniture.

Susan

I knew when Mum answered the phone that it was something awful. Her nose went funny and her voice changed.

'Oh, how nice to hear from…' she started.

'Oh? Oh, dear.'

'Oh, no!'

'Oh, how terrible.'

Long silence.

'I always thought he…' It was then she noticed me, listening from the doorway.

She had to tell me straight away when she put the phone down, because I was standing there.

'That was Miss Armstrong,' she said. 'It's about Jo.' She'd still got her hand on the receiver in its cradle, staring down at it. 'Pamela, Harold, Josephine. They've all been killed. They… They were in a car crash. At least they did all die together.' She looked up, out of the window. 'Rusty, too,' she added. She didn't look at me at all.

'I hope she got my birthday card,' I heard myself say.

Mum looked at me then. But as if she wasn't seeing me. 'Yes,' she said in a faraway voice. I don't think she'd even heard what I said.

That weekend, they said I wasn't to read the papers. Not that I ever did. They took the *News of the World* for the horoscopes, which Dad would read out loud. He read them as usual. After that the paper disappeared.

Jo was the first proper friend I had. She was my best friend and I was hers. I've learned that you can often say someone is your best friend, but it's risky to say that you are theirs, in case the feeling isn't as mutual as you thought. But with Jo, I knew I was safe to say it. We were at Miss Armstrong's school together.

I'll never forget the first time I met Miss Armstrong.

I am nine years old and shy, standing close to my dad in the hall of the house on Ridge Hill. The staircase with its polished banister curves up and up. Then she appears, coming down and down, as if on an escalator, tall and gaunt, fitting the proportions of the house exactly. She holds her head erect and looks down her long nose as she glides to our level.

Then she's striding towards us, hand outstretched, a warm smile lifting high cheekbones.

She shakes Dad's hand and turns with equal and terrifying courtesy to me.

Dad has come to interview Miss Armstrong to decide whether to send me to the school in her living room. But even I can tell that Miss Armstrong is the one doing the interviewing.

Miss Armstrong lives with her dog in a flat at the top of her sister's and brother-in-law's house. She and her sister are both alike and not alike. I've seen them striding about the town with hair scraped back in buns and no trace of make-up. But the sister is more rounded, mellower. Her husband, Mr Lawrence, is the librarian at Britannia Royal Naval College and teaches history there. He is soft of speech, wears a watch on a gold chain, moves slowly and whistles "S" sounds through his

Edwardian moustache. Although he is as gentle as the women of his household are fierce, I'm always scared to meet him because I can never understand a word he says.

The day after the phone call I had this conversation with my mother.

'When Miss Armstrong rang up,' I said. 'You know, to tell us. You said, "I always thought he…" Why did you say that?'

'I don't know what you're talking about.'

I was obstinate. I persisted. 'On the phone. You were talking to Miss Armstrong. You said "I always thought he…" What were you going to say? "I always thought he…" He *what*?'

I was thinking that maybe Jo's father was in one of his moods, driving too fast. Did he just go off the road? Turn the car over? Or was he overtaking and drove straight into another car? How did they "all die together", as my mother had said? Jo would have been in the back with Rusty. Did they hurtle forward? Fly through the windscreen? Land in a field? Did the ambulance come? Were they already dead? Did they die in hospital?

I didn't ask all these questions. I did ask where the crash happened, but Mum said she didn't know. She wouldn't talk about it. Eventually, she remembered what she said on the phone. 'I was going to say, "I always thought he drove rather fast".' That's all she would say. Questions were a no-go area.

'Don't think about it,' she said. 'You don't want to give yourself nightmares.'

A letter came from Miss Armstrong for me. I took it away to read in my room.

My Dear Susan,

I feel I must write you a few lines to say how dreadfully sorry I am that you should have lost Jo, a real friend of yours – and be feeling that sorrow which usually only comes when we are older and can better understand…

She went on about God's love and about Jo going with the parents she loved and being happier in heaven, which made me feel selfish for wanting her back. I read it over and over, but there was no further information. She even told me all about her holiday in Sark in the summer and the antics of the dogs, before signing off.

Do come and see me in the holidays.

Affectionately,
Ursula Armstrong

There was only one line that gave me a clue.

Thank the good Lord there was no one else involved.

So I guessed there wasn't another car. When I showed the letter to Mum, she nodded over that line and said, 'Yes indeed,' and her eyes welled up.

So, if there was no other vehicle involved, he must have been in a mood, and it would have been horrible in their car. It would have been very tense. The faster he drove, the more frightened Jo would have been. She'd have been trying to make it all right. Trying to say the right thing, when there wasn't a right thing to say.

The first morning at Miss Armstrong's school is daunting. I use the side entrance as instructed, but there is still the grand staircase to climb, past closed doors and family portraits. The top of the house smells of food cooking, but not the sort of food you'd want to eat. Miss Armstrong beckons me into the room, the dog barks and the other two pupils stare across the table.

I've just found my place in the history textbook when the dog, a black and tan mongrel called Dandy, starts to make strange noises beside my chair and then throws up on the carpet. My stomach heaves and I can feel my face burning. The other two giggle and nudge each other. I've never seen a dog being sick before and it's worse than I could have imagined. I just want the smelly mess to disappear but, instead of clearing it up, Miss Armstrong shovels ash from the grate over it. She explains that the ash will absorb the moisture and can be swept up later. I stare at the history book and keep swallowing. When I look up, Miss Armstrong is watching me with her head on one side, but says nothing.

Miss Armstrong has strong opinions, worships the Romans and hates maths. She is strict, but not in a frightening way, once you get used to her.

My classmates aren't as intimidating as they first appeared. Becky is the daughter of the Captain of the Naval College. She is the same age as me and, with both our fathers being in the Navy, we have something in common. Bobby lives in a boat on the river, which surprises me. I didn't even know you could do

26

that, and, anyway, he looks too ordinary. I soon learn that Miss Armstrong prefers boys to girls. She makes no bones about this fact. She finds boys more straightforward and less inclined to tears and cattiness. But Becky is her favourite of the three of us, because she is more of a tomboy than Bobby, even though he's actually a boy. Becky has two older brothers. Perhaps that's why she's a tomboy. I'd have found her frightening if she wasn't so straightforward and friendly.

When we're let out into the garden, Becky and I play "Hop-Along-Cassidy" in the bushes, taking it in turns to be the horse. In summer the school moves outside, either onto the verandah or onto the lawn. We roll about on the grass with Dandy, sneak the strawberries ripening against stones in the terraced vegetable garden and press our noses to the huge greenhouse to look at the grapevine.

When Josephine joins the school the next term I know immediately that I want her for a best friend. In the same instant I know that Becky isn't a best friend, even though we spend so much time together. I want to get to know Josephine, at the same time as feeling I already know her. There hasn't been any "getting to know" with Becky. What you see is what you get.

Josephine introduces herself as Jo. She has a self-possessed air, with her neat, practical clothes and short dark hair. Most other girls I know have their hair curled or plaited with ribbons and bows, but Jo has hers cut short. Instead of being belted and buttoned into dresses with Peter Pan collars, Jo is cool and crisp in cotton skirts and open-necked shirts.

Jo asks me to tea after school. She lives in a flat, but it isn't like our flat, which has an iron staircase to the front door and is all dark and pokey with ginger-grain paintwork that Mum hates.

Jo's flat is on the Kingswear side of the river, so we cross on the Lower Ferry, and the house is right round the corner from the slipway. Rusty greets Jo with an old, chewed slipper and they roll around on the floor until she remembers to introduce me. He's chestnut-coloured and a bit like a shaggy rug on legs, but very gentle and affectionate. Jo's mother is a smiley person who makes me feel at home straight away. She's a bit like Jo – neat features – but with curly auburn hair. The telephone keeps ringing and she answers it, "Pamela speaking," instead of saying the number like Mum. Pamela Kennedy obviously has a lot of friends. The flat is on the ground floor and there are steps into the river from the verandah. We can run straight out of the living room and go swimming. At least, Jo can. When I get home I say I have to learn to swim.

On Thursdays after school, Becky and I toil up the hill together in the heat to the College cricket ground. Our job is to score for the weekly cricket match. We clamber about behind the big green scoreboard, hanging the metal plates in place to display the score in black and white numbers. I learn to watch the game carefully and score accurately. We both consider it a disgrace if the official scorer has to beckon one of us over because we've displayed the wrong numbers. This role earns us the right to cricket tea in the marquee: cucumber sandwiches, sausage rolls. Sometimes we even get strawberries and cream. One week we try to take Jo with us, but Mr Pocket at the Lodge won't let her in and she goes off in a huff.

Miss Armstrong takes a broad view of education. She likes to be out of doors, so walks and picnics are a regular part of the timetable. She can outwalk any of us and has no patience with the modern trend towards "using the motor car at the drop of a hat".

28

'Soon,' she likes to predict, 'Children will be born without legs. They'll drop off if you don't use them.'

In order to prevent this happening we go on history walks, geography walks, wild flower walks and bird walks, all led by Miss Armstrong striding at great speed up the steep gradients and steps of the town and surrounding hills. She marches us up Crowther's Hill to Jawbones, and we make special expeditions across the river by Philip's ferry to toil up the hill to British Camp at Noss. Even Dandy protests when we do that in a heatwave and then have to listen to Miss Armstrong holding forth, yet again, about Iron Age hill forts. But at least it's downhill all the way home. For a treat, she takes us to see Danny Kaye in *Knock on Wood*. It's my first visit to the cinema and I laugh until I cry and then until I hurt and wish Danny Kaye would do something ordinary so that I can get my breath back.

One day, Jo comes with the news that her father, who owns the pottery at Warfleet, has invited us all to have a conducted tour. Mr Kennedy is very welcoming and introduces us to a nice lady who shows us around. We see the famous gurgle jugs and all the cups and plates with mottoes written on them, like *A rolling stone gathers no moss*. I keep wondering about that. Is moss a good thing, or not? If you are a stone, is it better to be smooth or furry? Both are nice. We watch the potters at work and touch the clay. It looks luscious like fudge, but it goes stiff as it dries. I have to keep washing my hands all day to get it out of my skin.

Jo is very excited because they are leaving the flat in Kingswear next week. She can't wait to move into the new house over on our side of the river, which has a big garden with barns

29

and a field and woods. It's just up the hill from the pottery. 'So that Daddy will be able to walk to work,' she says. 'You'll have to come and play.' I'm looking forward to that.

It was difficult to be properly sad when nobody would talk about Jo's death. It felt like crying wasn't allowed. I found a poem by Tennyson that helped.

> *Break, break, break*
> *On thy cold gray stones, O sea!*

I could relate that to the waves at Sugary Cove where we used to go for picnics with Miss Armstrong. The phrase, "the tender grace of a day that is dead" conjured the magic of that time as well as its abrupt end. I would read the whole thing over and over again, repeating the lines:

> *But O for the touch of a vanish'd hand*
> *And the sound of a voice that is still!*

until they produced tears. It made me feel better until I started wondering whether that made me a hypocrite.

Pamela

It all started with being listened to.

No, that's not right. It all started with being seen. The listening came later.

It was that first evening at your house that it happened.

It's early spring and I've brought a bunch of primroses. There's quite a party, at least two other couples. I find Bunny busy in the kitchen and she gives me a cream jug for the flowers. It fits them perfectly, and I put them on the coffee table.

'My favourites,' you say, handing me a gin and tonic.

'Mine, too. They smell so green. Like spring.' I look up as I tweak the flowers and our eyes meet.

It's like slipping into another dimension, a magic room almost, with just the two of us inside it. Like a bee might feel inside a snapdragon, sipping nectar. It only lasts seconds.

'I told Bunny I'd give her a hand,' I say and go back to the kitchen.

In bed that night, lying next to my husband, instead of sleeping I find I am looking into your eyes. It's like the spiritual rush of my first communion, and it's like sex. Innocent, yet it makes me feel guilty. Did you even share the moment?

I've known Bunny for some time. We both volunteer at the hospital – wheeling the book trolley round, helping with the teas and chatting to patients who don't have visitors. Sometimes we meet up for a coffee in the Bay Tree when we're shopping on a Friday morning. I've been to her house a couple of times for meetings, but I never met you there. It turns out that Harold knows you through the sailing club. You've crewed for him on occasion.

Not long after that first dinner party Josephine comes down with chicken pox. I ring Miss Armstrong in the morning to say she won't be in school. Then I ring Bunny as I won't be going to the hospital. She says calamine lotion is good for the spots, do I have any? I don't. She says you're coming our way and she'll send you with a bottle.

When I open the door you're standing there with the pink bottle in your hand. Normally, you would hand it over, go on your way. But I'm so grateful. And I feel as if I've always known you. It seems entirely natural to invite you in. I give you coffee at the kitchen table. Mrs H is peeved, I can tell, because I have my chat with you that morning, instead of with her.

'Sorry if I stink of Jeyes fluid,' you say. 'I was scrubbing out the greenhouse over the weekend. It's a devil, getting rid of the smell.'

'Greenhouse? You have one? I was thinking that would be nice – to have one. I was sowing tomato seed.' I indicate the seed trays on the kitchen windowsill.

You grow tomatoes from seed as well, and we discuss which varieties we've tried. Josephine comes down in her dressing gown to see who's visiting and has a glass of Lucozade. You tell her that, when you had chicken pox, the spots were all over your head.

'I only found out when I combed my hair.' You demonstrate by running your fingers through your hair and making an agony face, which makes Josephine laugh.

Thick hair. It bounces back. I want to touch it.

*

A week or so later I'm walking Rusty at Little Dartmouth. It's just after sunrise and the light on the water is startling. I lean on the gate for a while, hypnotised by golden ripples stretching across to Start Point. Then I dip down to walk along the cliff tops. It's where I go to refuel, to let the sea work its magic. Where we live you'd never know the river was so close, let alone the sea. It was better in the Kingswear flat. The sea was out of sight, but I could smell it, see the rise and fall of the tide in the river and hear the power of it, slapping up against the garden wall. I liked it there with neighbours, shops and the ferry to Dartmouth just round the corner. But I love this house and garden, of course I do. The valley is a mass of greenery and birdsong. It's peaceful and beautiful, but it's the sea I need. I'll sit for hours watching the waves breaking on the Dancing Beggars. You can see how they got their name. In a heavy swell, if you keep gazing, it's as if the raggedy-jaggedy rocks are cavorting in the spray that is crashing around them. But I can't hang about this morning. I call Rusty, who has his nose down a rabbit hole, and keep on up the valley.

One section of the path is laid with stone slabs, which stops it turning into a mudslide. The stones are interleaved, unevenly embedded and worn into hollows by weather and feet. I fall to wondering who has trodden the path before me. Fishermen or farmers, maybe, struggling to make a living. Coastguards on the lookout for smugglers. Fugitives escaping the revenue men. What urgency or weariness have these stones absorbed?

Just as I'm about to turn back I feel a vibration in the ground, which turns into the sound of footsteps. Someone running, slowing to a walk. And there you are, striding towards me.

'Oh!' I say.

That is all I can manage. You fill the gap, saying that you, too, enjoy this time of day.

'Keeps me sane. Clears my head before work,' you say, making a fuss of Rusty.

As we stand there, yards apart, I feel a jolt of energy through the soles of my feet – as if you have sent it through the packed earth via some underground conduit.

To come upon you so unexpectedly, to be alone together – these circumstances are unnerving. I'm afraid to meet those eyes of yours. We both fall back on remarks about the weather, point out the primroses in the bank, focus on the buzzard soaring overhead.

'I could sit on a rock, watching the sea, for hours,' you say. 'Not that I have hours.' You look at your watch. 'In fact I'd better be heading back.'

Without thinking, I fall into step with you. As we walk, the talking becomes easier, even when we have to walk one behind the other. Or just because of that. Rusty falls behind and then thunders after us, weaving back and forth between us. At Deadman's Cove we pause and stare out to sea, until I realise you aren't staring out to sea. You are staring at me. We clamber up to the woodland path, where bluebell spikes are beginning to push up between their dark leaves. When we reach the road we meet another dog-walker, which prompts me to check the time. What have I been thinking of? I'll never get back to my car in time to get home, make breakfast and get Josephine off to school.

'That's okay,' you say. 'I'll drop you off. Won't take five minutes.'

I hold Rusty between my knees to stop him jumping into the back and getting mud on the seats. At Little Dartmouth we pass a man in a tractor and you raise a hand in greeting. You even wait to make sure my car starts.

When I get home, Harold isn't yet downstairs and Josephine is feeding the hens. I take the porridge out of the Aga, plug in the coffee percolator and lay the table with the mottoware from the pottery, which we always use for breakfast. *Look before you leap*, proclaims the milk jug as I fill it.

Alone in the kitchen, that 'Oh!' with which I greeted you comes back to me. It said far too little in terms of what was socially acceptable; and far too much in terms of what should have stayed inside my head. Even alone in the kitchen, my face burns to think of it.

'Lovely morning,' I say when Harold appears. As I make the toast, I wonder why I don't tell him about bumping into you. I look from the milk jug to my plate, which tells me that *He who hesitates is lost*. Josephine is always questioning these apparent contradictions.

'If I look before I leap, then I'll hesitate, and I'll be lost,' she says one Sunday morning.

'They're about two different things entirely,' says Harold. '*Look before you leap*, that's about planning. *He who hesitates* is about timing. Both crucial skills. When we were rally driving—'

Josephine interrupts. 'Was that the Jabberwock team?' She knows it was, of course, but she loves saying that word.

Harold nods, impatient. 'As I was saying, when we were rallying, for instance, we'd always study the course beforehand, as a team, recce it if we had the chance – looking before we leapt. Then we'd work out a strategy, a race plan. All very deliberate. But when you're actually behind the wheel, you have to seize the moment, rely on your instinct. Otherwise you're a dead man.

It's all about timing, split-second decisions. If you hesitate then you're bound to be lost.'

The two sides of my husband neatly summed up, I think as I pour him more coffee. The methodical businessman and the daredevil risk-taker. Josephine doesn't contradict her father, but later, when we're washing up, she says she thinks it's more to do with different types of people.

'Like Ginny at school. You'd say to her *Look before you leap*, because then maybe she'd think before she opened her mouth and she wouldn't keep getting into trouble. But with Susan, who's so cautious, you'd say, *He who hesitates is lost*. Except you'd have to say, *She who hesitates*.'

Good thinking for an eleven-year-old. Josephine can be such a tomboy, but she's thoughtful too. I used to be a tomboy, but I never analysed things like she does. 'Yes,' I say. 'You're right. That's another way of looking at it.'

She adds, 'All that about planning and timing… It's very Daddy.'

That makes me smile, and it sets me thinking about you. That perfect timing of our first meeting on the coast path. We happen to meet surprisingly often after that first encounter. Is that just coincidence? Or does it involve planning and timing? I like to think it's chance. It's too tempting to think you may be contriving to bump into me.

That's when the listening starts. You want to know what the trouble is. You can see there is trouble. You see past the happy family togetherness, the hostess smiles. You want to understand, and recommend daily doses of tender loving care, as if I can get it on prescription. I explain that sometimes it's as if Harold uses up all the air in the room, and that I am the only one who administers the loving care in our house.

'I can understand that,' you say. 'There's a stillness in you. It would steady him.'

'Stillness?' I'm surprised at how shrill I sound and you look round with raised eyebrows.

That little exchange – so few words – causes me so much distress. I've told you I'm struggling for air and that is your response. Stillness, indeed. Commotion is what I carry inside me. I've overestimated you and I'm disappointed. I suppose I imagined you could read my mind. How could you? We hardly know each other. I decide to dismiss you from my thoughts.

But I encounter you again one day at Little Dartmouth. It's a stormy morning in late April, a south-westerly gale. Rusty is cantering in all directions with the wind in his ears.

'Come on,' you say and start running down the steep hill from the stile.

I get caught up in the moment. I start to run, can't stop, careering down the slope over stones and gullies and tussocks of grass, faster and faster, exhilarated by the rake of the wind in my hair, the fierce sting of air on my cheeks and the needling of rain in my eyes as it sweeps in off the sea. I feel like a kid again. You're laughing, ready to catch me, but I swerve aside and gallop on, gradually slowing to a halt where Rusty is waiting for me to come to my senses.

My headscarf has slipped back and is round my neck, and my hair is all over the place. That's when you say it.

'I've never seen you like that before – spontaneous. You're always so… I don't know. You just never let go. You should do it more often.'

'Hardly,' I say, turning into the wind to reposition the headscarf. 'I mean, it wouldn't be appropriate, would it?' I tie it with a double knot under my chin.

You just sigh and shake your head. As we walk on I think how shocked Harold would have been to see me running like that. And on the way home I mentally forgive you. Maybe you do understand. Not that it makes any difference. There's no room for my commotion.

Gradually, of course, it all comes out. Not just the worries about Harold, but how it is affecting me. I tell you about the meningitis.

'He depends on me, you see. To manage the moods, the migraines.'

'Migraines I can understand. But moods?'

'I know. I don't understand either. Just that they are there and I know how... Let's just say, he married his nurse and I've never stopped being one. Not really.'

'His nurse?'

'That's how we met. Didn't you know? But why should you? After the meningitis – he was very ill. I was a newly qualified nurse and he was on my ward. He came out of hospital just before Christmas 1941. We got married in the February.'

'Right in the middle of the war.'

'I suppose he was lucky. He was invalided out of the army. Went into business and I carried on nursing until Josephine arrived.'

'Hmm. And the business? He manages that?'

'Oh, yes. He takes great pride in it. When Harold got into all his speed addictions his father wrote him off as a tearaway. Ironic, really. Especially as his father bankrolled the flying and the rally

38

driving in the first place. And Harold's turned into the reliable businessman – he's more than proved himself. In contrast to his father, who kept making and losing fortunes. Other people's fortunes, as it happened. You knew he committed suicide?'

You nod. 'To avoid prison, I believe?'

'Yes. Harold likes to think people don't know. He felt publicly disgraced. As to his mother, he never talks about her, not since his father died. He never even sees her these days. And she's never taken the slightest interest in Josephine.'

It's a relief to talk about those things. And you listen. It's nothing to begin with. Just the listening.

You are a good friend and you have your finger on my pulse, so to speak.

The warm smile, the firm handshake, the kindness in your eyes. It means the world to me. To be heard. To be noticed. To be cared for.

It's around that time that Miss Armstrong gets the children to do an end-of-term show for the parents. The school now has new premises, and she's obviously proud of how it's expanded. There's an exhibition of work laid out on tables, some pictures stuck up on the walls and tea and biscuits being handed round. Then we all sit down to listen. One of the younger ones plays a recorder piece – only one, thankfully. The rest of the children recite poetry they've learned by heart. Josephine makes her way through "Drake's Drum" with only one hiccup.

'Thank goodness we won't be testing her on that any more,' I say as I tell you the story. 'Next came a girl called Ginny, a friend of Josephine's. She'd just got started on that poem about a rider in the woods by—'

'Walter de la Mare,' you interrupt. '"*Is there anybody there? said the Traveller.*"'

'Exactly!' I say, surprised. 'But just wait. She was just going on, "*Knocking on the moonlit door,*" when there came a rapping on the door and a man appeared. "Come to read the gas meter," he said. Of course, it brought the house down! After that Ginny couldn't get past those first two lines. Miss Armstrong had to tell her to start at the bit about the horse.'

We have a good laugh. It still makes me giggle to think of the gas man knocking and poor Ginny's face.

'Poor girl,' you said. 'Must have been hard – especially as it's really such a sad poem.'

I nod as if I understand. But the poem was new to me and, in the general hilarity, I didn't take that in at the time. It makes me feel rather shallow, and I resolve to look it up when I'm next in the library.

You seem to pop up everywhere. We meet in the baker's when I'm buying bread and you've just nipped out for a pasty for your lunch. Another day you surprise me in Cundell's. I'm being served and I'm miles away, watching the rashers of bacon fall neatly from the slicing machine. As the lady sets them on the scales, I catch sight of you watching me through the window.

Forgetting that I intended to buy sausages as well, I hurry to pay and leave the shop. But you've gone. I pretend not to be disappointed and go into Dawes' for bread. When I come out you're waiting on Wise's corner.

'I like your dress,' you say.

'This? I've had it ages.' It's just a cotton shirtwaister with a pattern of leaves, what my mother would call a washing dress.

'It suits you. It's all swirly.'

I laugh, embarrassed. 'It's nice and cool.' Behind us, the church clock begins to strike the hour. 'Goodness! Is that the time?' I check my watch. 'Eleven already. I must get on.'

I leave you standing there, clutching your newspaper, and hurry along to Lloyds Bank.

Sometimes when we're at your house for dinner, you hang back as we move into the dining room, so that your gaze can say things that can never be spoken. Fortunately, Harold never notices. Harold is a jealous man. He doesn't trust women.

Early on, I learned to be careful around men because of that, and I've forgotten the power I used to possess. When I was nursing, it happened all the time – doctors falling at my feet, one of them quite literally. I broke a few hearts when I married Harold.

I first met him as "the stroppy one in Bed 7". So I wasn't expecting to fall in love. He was impatient, abrasive even, but in a comical way. Maybe the other nurses didn't get his sense of humour. It was a breath of fresh air to me – which was welcome over a bedpan and a blanket bath. Later, I realised it was his way of coping with the embarrassment. A young man, good-looking, who'd been struck down and found himself at the mercy of young nurses – the sort of girls he'd have met at a party, invited out. Also, he had no wounds or dramatic tale to be reticent about. I think that made him feel inferior, as if he didn't have the same right to care as the war heroes. But he'd been really ill. I flicked through his notes when he was asleep and Sister wasn't looking. He nearly didn't make it at all.

But now he was on the mend and getting stronger by the week, as was our friendship. I got reprimanded more than once for spending too much time on that particular patient. After the third warning I was moved to Men's Surgical and we had to rely on my friend, Betty, as go-between, passing notes back and forth. Betty was a good sort. We shared a room in the nurses' home and had been on several light-hearted double dates together. She had misgivings about Harold. 'He's a firebrand, that one,' she told me. 'You might find you've bitten off more than you can chew.' I pooh-poohed Betty's concerns. How could she possibly tell, with Harold confined to a hospital ward and inventing tall stories, no doubt, to impress us both? She was going steady by then with a houseman who was very earnest and very boring. No wonder she found Harold's attitude intimidating. It was nothing I couldn't handle.

My parents' farm was the perfect place to convalesce. I wangled leave and ensconced him there to build his strength on the eggs, butter and meat that were unavailable in town. He claimed not to have any family, which I later discovered was untrue. His parents lived rather grandly in Belgravia, but he preferred to come to my home. At the time I was flattered. It was only much later that I realised this said every bit as much about his relationship with his parents as it did about his attraction to me.

Pamela, the caring nurse, turned into the adoring fiancée, the attentive wife, the competent housekeeper, the loving mother. We got married so quickly and Josephine was born eighteen months later. Sometimes I almost believed Harold was jealous of her when she was a baby. Is that possible? He's devoted to her now, of course. They do so much together. But when she was little, I was so focused on her, as any mother is on her baby. It took my attention away from him. I suppose that was it. He withdrew and I shrivelled. Maybe it's just as well that I can't have another.

I've never taken to sailing, but Harold and Josephine have always loved to sail. This year, when the season starts, you and Harold set up a weekend cruise to Salcombe. When we set off the sea is calm, but there's enough breeze to send us skimming along.

Harold tinkers about with the engine, which he loves to do. Bunny and I chat, and you and Josephine take it in turns at the helm. During your spell, you tease me for failing to get the foresail properly set. It sounds overfamiliar, and I turn my back.

You behave yourself after that, but it's strange for us all to be sleeping in such close proximity, with all the issues of guarding privacy and decorum that that involves. I'm afraid the telepathy crackling between us may be clearly audible, and that the electricity I feel will give Harold a shock when he touches me. It's rough on the way back and we tease you about living up to your nickname and bringing bad weather. I pretend to feel more ill than I do and take to my bunk. The truth is, I'm exhausted by the effort of avoiding eye contact with you.

I still share duties with Bunny at the hospital, of course. She's different from most of my friends – more like an older sister. We swap recipes and books. That is, she lets me have her recipes with all sorts of extra tips she's worked out for herself, and I lend her magazines and my favourite novels. For instance, Bunny enjoys the humour in *One Pair of Feet* – I love Monica Dickens, and especially that one, as it's about nursing. But the more romantic ones aren't to her taste. She prefers biographies or whodunits and is working her way through the library's Agatha Christie collection. She likes finding books for Josephine and introduces her to Arthur Ransome. *Swallows and Amazons* is right up her street.

Occasionally Bunny asks my advice about clothes – she's got no fashion sense whatsoever. We have a session looking though her wardrobe.

'We must get you out of all this navy blue,' I say.

'But it matches my hair. That's what I was told.'

I've always envied the swing and shine of Bunny's perfectly straight hair. 'Your hair is wonderful – so dark and shiny – but it isn't navy blue!'

We both laugh, which is a relief because I'm having a problem not looking at the neatly made bed where you and she must sleep, side by side. I suppose I'd hoped to see twin beds. Bunny is telling me that she's always been baffled by this chance remark about her hair, which she took to heart and which has shaped her wardrobe ever since.

I take her on a shopping spree to Plymouth soon after that and persuade her to buy a candy-striped blouse with a big collar. The crisp pink lifts her whole appearance. I don't think it's my imagination – people take more notice of what Bunny says in meetings when she's wearing it. I count it a personal triumph, even though she wears it with a navy skirt.

It never occurs to me that Bunny would mind my encounters and conversations with you. If I think about it at all, I believe she'd be glad for me. On the other hand, I never mention them to her.

But one day Bunny jolts me out of my complacency. We're having morning coffee in the Bay Tree when she digs into her shopping bag and produces a well-worn copy of *Treasure Island*.

'I thought Josephine might like to borrow it. I discovered it when I was her age and read it over and over.'

I take the book from her and study the dust jacket.

Before I can thank her, Bunny goes on, 'I could be very jealous of you...'

Her words slice into me like a hot knife. When I look up, her grey eyes are gazing at me steadily. In that moment I have a flash of knowing that I have been taking Bunny for granted, assuming she would indulge me. But no, she is not my older sister. She is just like any other wife in laying claim to her husband.

Bunny continues in her matter-of-fact tone. 'You see, we couldn't have children, me and Jonah. I wanted to adopt, but he would have none of it. So, you see, Josephine is special to me and I'm grateful to be something of an auntie to her.'

'Oh, Bunny,' I start, but she shakes her head.

'I don't want to dwell on it. But I wanted you to know. Now, where have those teacakes got to?'

In the days that follow, that phrase, 'could be very jealous of you', keeps coming back to me. How calculated was the pause that followed it? Were her eyes searching mine with intent? What did they see? Was she hinting that she might have reason to be jealous of more than Josephine? I tell myself that Bunny's not like that. She isn't one for a hidden agenda. Even so, it feels like a warning.

Nevertheless, all through the summer, when it gets light so early, we meet as I walk Rusty. But now I keep to my own route and we make sure we are never seen together. There is little we don't discuss, from your taste in poetry to the state of the world or black spot on roses.

You know so much about poetry, even if it is only from studying it at school. Your teacher must have been stricter than mine. You can tell me whole sonnets, Wordsworth mostly.

Also, Browning's "Home-Thoughts, from Abroad", which is a favourite of mine. I like Keats, but I can't even manage a whole verse of the poems I claim to know. They've stayed in my mind in pictures – the bitter cold conjured in "The Eve of St Agnes", the rich colours of the casement in Madeline's chamber, the jewels and fruits, and then the carpets rising along the "gusty floor".

You introduce me to Yeats and give me a copy of his selected works for my birthday. You've bookmarked "When You Are Old". It takes me a while to understand why you picked that poem. I hide the little book in a shoebox.

You're very keen on your roses. One day you're explaining how one of them isn't flowering properly.

'It's *Lady Sylvia*. She comes into bud and you can see the petals – that lovely pink ready to emerge. And then – nothing.'

You stop suddenly on the path, looking down at me.

'I've just realised…'

I frown. You're looking at me so strangely.

'It's like you – you've never really bloomed, have you? Sad.' You turn away abruptly and walk on.

I stand, looking out to sea, blinking back tears. I feel as if I've been slapped.

After a while, I hear footsteps and your arm comes across my shoulders.

'I'm sorry,' you say. 'I had no right to say such a thing.'

'I'm perfectly happy,' I say.

'I know,' you say.

Your words come back to me as I'm making pastry for a pie that afternoon. You named something I don't want to know about myself, a need I refuse to admit to. 'I'm perfectly happy,'

I repeat to myself as I furiously rub flour into lard, eliminating the squidgy lumps and creating the required texture of fine breadcrumbs.

I suppose Harold misses the rallying. He wanted to get back to it, but the doctors said no. The tension, the excitement, the challenges of rallying, spread over hours, could trigger a seizure that, at the wheel, could be fatal. Normal driving, short distances, shouldn't be a problem, they said. In any case the team broke up, and several of his mates were killed in action over France. But he kept that car, the V8. He was always more in love with that than he was with me. It frightens me. Especially since that day in late June.

'We'll just go for a spin,' he says.

I know what he has in mind – to drive out to Strete Gate and along Slapton Sands to Torcross. He always treats the Slapton line like a runway – putting his foot down, leaning forward, muttering to himself, then leaning back as if he expects the car to take off. It's a grey day and there aren't many people about on the beach. No parked cars to get in the way. As he gathers speed, I hold my hands in my lap, careful not to clench them, but squeezing my right thumb for luck. My foot is nearly through the floor as we approach the village.

"Brake now!" I'm screaming inside my head. He'll never make the bend.

Torcross is busy. Cars parked by the shops. A couple feeding the ducks by the Ley on the right. A family emerging from the left – mother pushing a pram, father holding a small child by the hand. I take all this in as we hurtle towards them.

Then the child sees the ducks, points and starts forward,

pulling away from his father's hand.

'Stop!' The sound escapes from my throat as a strangled squawk.

A violent swerve, and we are past them. I see a flash of blue as the child is grabbed back, the father's wide eyes, his snarling mouth.

'Clown! Damn fools! That'll teach that kid to look out.' Harold flexes his fingers, holding the wheel with his thumbs. The vein at his temple is throbbing. 'Really, Pamela! Whatever was the matter? Everything perfectly under control. With reflexes like mine…'

I dare not say a thing. He might drive us straight into the Ley. I look round at Josephine, who is silent behind us. She stares back with huge eyes, all colour drained from her face.

At times like that I have a glimpse of how he used to be, getting his pilot's licence, addicted to speed, revelling in his skill. A tearaway, not a domestic animal. He never grew up. He grew ill, instead. What with that and the War, he never had a chance.

But it's not as if he's trapped. He gets to travel. Takes satisfaction in the business, being bold with new lines, hiring the most skilled workers. But he does have a temper. I have to work very hard to keep the moods at bay and to make our little family unit a happy one. That comment of yours comes back to me, along with the feel of the wind in my hair, the energy of it. 'You never let go,' you said. Of course I never let go.

Now, of course, he adores Josephine. Treats her more like a son, and she's always risen to every challenge. I wonder, though, about her growing up. She's already getting more feminine, interested in girl's things. He may find that difficult.

And how will he cope with boyfriends? It won't be long now. She's a popular girl.

Spring-cleaning this year reflects what's happening inside me. I see the world with such clarity, like the view through freshly polished windows – brighter colours of sparkling intensity, sharper feelings, heightened sensuality. Anticipation, disappointment, surprise, joy, pain – they all helter-skelter through me while I continue to peel potatoes and iron shirts. Unlike spring-cleaning, the effect lasts through the summer months. While my hands are busy at practical tasks, my mind takes me into a dreamland. Sometimes I hardly know the difference between what really happens and what I imagine.

There's the time I'm alone in the house in a late summer storm. Harold is in New York on business and Josephine is staying with Mum. They get on so well, it's become a September tradition. Mum takes her to a show in London and they go to Liberty's – all sorts of treats before school starts again.

Usually I love to have the house to myself. But this time I'm restless. The wind gets up and sets the old beams creaking. The rain is lashing down and I'm sad for the dahlias, which will be shredded. An elbow of wisteria knocks so hard on the kitchen window frame that I go to the door to make sure there's nobody there.

I bank up the fire and settle with a book but that knocking has set my imagination going. Suppose that was you, I think. Broken down on the road, water in the engine. Or your path blocked by a fallen tree. I would bring you in and give you cocoa or brandy. Probably both. I would run a bath to warm you up and take your clothes to dry them across the fire.

My imagination won't stop there. It draws you into my arms – damp and smelling of Imperial Leather. It leads us into the spare bedroom. Darkness warm as silk. We're so used to talking, but there are no words now, no questions. No looking either. Only touch and taste and smell. We slide between crisp sheets as if slipping into another time and space.

A coal shifts and the fire falls in on itself, sending fireflies into the soot on the fireback. I stir up the embers to release the last of the heat and light a cigarette. I blow a smoke ring and watch it fade. It's a relief that I won't be hurrying to strip the spare bed, hiding the sheets, glad that tomorrow is laundry day, and that the man will collect the box in the morning. I smile at myself. Crazy woman. My prosaic, sensible self won't even allow me a fantasy without tying up all the practical ends. I throw the cigarette into the fire and go to fill a hot water bottle.

Imagination is a dangerous thing, I think as I wait for the kettle to boil. Several times lately Harold has caught me daydreaming.

'You were miles away,' he said, and I felt reprimanded.

It won't do. I must be careful. He doesn't like my attention elsewhere.

The wind and rain has eased a little. Maybe the dahlias will survive after all. Tomorrow I'll cut back that wisteria branch.

Next day I banish my day-dreamy self and focus on being purposeful and domestic in preparation for Harold's return. A casserole in the Aga, his silver cigarette box gleaming, a fire alight in welcome. I'm ironing Harold's shirts when I fall to wondering how much I really know of the man who lives and breathes inside them every day – that is, how much I know beyond his insistence that they be immaculately pressed.

It's when I sprinkle the collar with water and it sizzles under the hot soleplate of the iron... The steam releases the unmistakeable smell of Harold, which has resisted all the soap and water and which I used to find so attractive. I swear I could identify him by that smell in a blindfold test, but today it evokes only affection, fondness. It no longer arouses me. Harold wasn't my first lover and he wasn't the best, but in the early days we were both as much in lust as we were in love. Once we were married he became demanding. He wanted it all the time. "Little and often" is how I thought of him in those days. But I taught him a thing or two, enough at least to make sure my own needs were met.

I thought I knew the man inside out, but realise now that knowledge simply consists of endless facts – requirements for his comfort that shape my life. Something else must go on in his head. In his heart. I have no idea what. And he certainly doesn't know what goes on in my head, which is just as well. Is the man I fell in love with still in there? What makes him like he is? One minute full of charm and fun, the next brooding, angry, threatening even?

When we met, it was all about those physical requirements. He was ill and I was his nurse. Maybe it just became a habit. Maybe it was his illness I fell in love with. That nurse's instinct to make it better. That's what Mother thought. "At least wait until he's fully fit again, Pammy. Then see if you still love him." I just laughed and shrugged off her concerns. Of course I would still love him. And there was a war on, so we rushed into it. I met all his friends. We had such fun! Everyone partying to take their minds off the bombs and the horror. Then came Josephine, and Harold became completely absorbed in establishing himself in business. He never wanted to talk of the past and I didn't press him for fear of upsetting him. Now I come to think of it, we never did take the time to get to know each other.

I shake out the last shirt and drape it over a hanger to air. If only I could hang them in his dressing room just as they are. You'd think that would be convenient – all ready to put on. But no. Harold insists they are folded. So I start the tedious business of buttoning each shirt. I suspect this is how his father liked his shirts, but Harold would never admit it. Odd relationship with his parents. I rarely saw them together, but he was never relaxed. Not like when I go home and flop. I know that Mum will look after me and spoil me a bit. Of course I help her out with things, but it's give and take. But Harold was always buying his mother flowers and chocolates – almost as if he was courting her. She certainly never ironed shirts. She would have sent them to the laundry. But Harold likes them done by hand – not his hand, of course. He imagines it all happens by magic – if he thinks of it at all.

As to his father, Harold would be angry with him behind his back, but to his face he was always out to impress, as if he needed his approval. Which made no sense. Because Harold said his father's business was little more than a criminal activity. Which, of course, it turned out to be.

I straighten up and stretch to ease my back. Harold will be home soon. What sort of mood will he be in? Only three more shirts.

Harold was furious when his father died. There was no grieving. He just went on about the shame. Not just on account of the fraud, that was bad enough, but the suicide. "Bringing shame on the family." That was all Harold seemed to care about. He was mad at his mother for defending her husband. 'Mother's no better than he was,' he told me. I think that upset him most of all. It sent him into such a black mood. You can't help wondering what sort of childhood he had with parents like that.

I fold the last of the shirts and add it to the pile. I place them on the shelf in his wardrobe. They look as neat as if they were new, but without the pins.

I slip off my comfortable slacks and pull on my new Viyella shirtwaister – Harold prefers me in a dress. It's a soft grey check and I'm pleased with it – light but warm, good for this in-between season. I'll wear it on Saturday. Bunny's invited us to dinner. I want you to see me in it. I think you'll like it. I'm just fastening the last suspender when I hear a toot-toot as Harold parks his car. Relief. He's coming home in a good mood. I hurry down to put out the ice for the gin and tonic.

After downing the first stiff gin, he wants me there and then on the hearthrug in front of the welcome fire.

'Take off your knickers,' is all he says.

With Josephine away, there's nothing to stop us. It's the last thing I want, but I don't want to spoil his mood and find I'm quickly aroused in spite of myself. Maybe it's the element of the unexpected or the flickering warmth on my skin. I start off imagining I'm with you on the grass in the corner of a field just off the cliff path. But I end up responding to my husband and getting powerfully carried away. It takes me quite by surprise.

The good mood comes to an abrupt end on Saturday night. Harold hardly utters a word on the way home from Bunny's dinner. There was a moment, just before the meal, when I thought he had one of his heads coming on. I offer to drive, but he declines.

I natter on about pruning the wisteria and Bunny's casserole.

'Shin, she said it was. Got it from Luscombe's. She often goes there. Such a cheap cut, but you'd never know. Just have to cook it twice as long.'

Harold grunts.

'Tender, wasn't it?'

He looks sideways at me and I smell the brandy on his breath.

I try again. 'Did you notice their new rug? I wasn't sure about the colour in that room.'

No reply. Only the revving of the engine as we swing round a bend too fast.

The flick-flack of the wipers fills the silence and I begin to wonder what I've said, what I've done. I replay the conversation at the table, trying to recall who said what. I can remember what you said, of course, and get diverted, rerunning the glances that passed between us. Flick-flack and Harold's breathing, heavier than usual. There was that remark about shooting rats. The emphasis he put on it. What was that all about?

Screech of brakes, blare of a horn as we swerve past another car in the narrows. I catch my breath, fearful that my gasp will sound deafening in the silence hanging between us.

'Damn fool!'

The words bounce off the windscreen.

'Damn, bloody fool!' Harold shouts this time. He's not addressing the other driver. He means me. What am I supposed to have done?

At home, he parks the car outside the barn doors as usual and turns off the ignition. But he doesn't get out. We both sit there, staring out at the blackness beyond the windscreen. The only sound is the tick of hot metal as the engine starts to cool.

In the house I offer tea, but he prefers whisky. He suggests I go on up to bed. But he follows almost immediately. He throws himself on top of me, squeezing my breasts, biting my neck, inflicting pain. He's hurt me before, especially in the early days, but then it felt accidental, a side effect of his passion. Tonight it is without doubt the object of the exercise.

In the muddy, dog-walking world, we continue to walk and talk. Nothing can come of it. You are married. So am I. We are all friends. You are an honourable man. I am a loyal wife and devoted mother. Bunny is my friend.

What exactly is this thing that started with being seen and grew into being heard, this "it" that I crave? Your attention? Your admiration? Is it simply warmth? You flicked some kind of switch inside me. You are in my head all the time. Your eyes, your smile. They comfort me. I can fall asleep if I imagine you holding my hand. Deep down, I know what "it" is and I dare not name it.

We are very chaste. The most prolonged physical contact we ever have is in full view of our spouses and all our friends – at the Regatta Ball. Harold is on the organising committee, and is expected to make up a table. It's etiquette, of course, for every man to dance with every lady in the party. You whisper in my ear that you wish you could dance with me all evening. It's the nearest you come to a declaration of feelings that does not involve your eyes. I make sure we don't dance together again. I know Harold will be watching me closely.

It's innocent, I tell myself. Yet, as I lie awake beside Harold in the small hours, I know that this innocent activity is as much a betrayal of my marriage as if you and I had been coupling like rabbits, the rabbits we often send scuttling into their burrows among the bracken on the cliff top. It's like sex for the soul. Can it stay that way? Or is it only a matter of time? I feel guilty of the things we don't do, because, in my fantasy world, I have indeed committed those sins. I justify my behaviour in my head on the grounds that it makes me a better wife, a happier mother. I have more energy. I sleep better. Except for the nights when I do not sleep at all.

Opportunities to be innocent together are limited. We know there will be gossip if we are seen. And gossip assumes guilt. Gossip is not interested in innocence. It will curdle innocence in the blink of a curious eye. What feels almost sacred to us will turn sordid in the words of the world. So we are careful.

There comes a time when the few risks we take flip from being exciting to being frightening. The anxiety involved in keeping a rendezvous almost eclipses the joy of meeting and quickly runs into the pain of parting, so that any euphoria quickly evaporates. Delight in each other's company is losing its shine. We both know at some unspoken level that the relationship is doomed.

This morning I steeled myself.

'We mustn't do this any more.' I said it as soon as we met, before we had even touched. 'It's too dangerous. I must never see you alone again.'

And so it has ended. I may have said the words, but you met them so readily that I knew it was already in your mind and almost on your own lips. Deep inside me I'm disappointed that you concurred so readily. I wanted you to put up a fight for us. But my practical, responsible self knows that would only have made it harder.

I've imagined other ways forward. Of course I have. The "What-if" questions. What if it were to become more than a friendship? What if you and I decided to make a life together? But when I think about confessing – how it would destroy Harold, how devastated Josephine would be… It's unthinkable. Anyway, I love Harold. Is it possible to love two people? I love Harold unconditionally. Or is that something I tell myself, because it was true once? I silence that uncomfortable inner voice. I plighted my troth all those years ago – for better for worse, till death us do part. I keep my promises, so it must be true. True or not, it's hard work, but I still believe it's love. What is love? Why do we have so few words for it? Harold adores me and depends upon me, but he does not love me. I know that now.

You and I both know how we feel. We both know it cannot be. That is all there is to it. I hold the glow of your final hug like a cloak around me.

Harold is on edge tonight. He grabbed the whisky bottle the moment he came in, and then dragged me off for a drink at the Sportsman's Arms before we fetched Josephine from swimming. Now he's settled to read the news. The vein on his temple is throbbing and the muscle in his cheek is jumping. He catches my eye round the edge of the paper.

'What are you looking at me like that for?'

'No reason. I didn't mean…'

'Is there anything you want to tell me?'

My scalp moves and it seems to be snowing inside my head.

'I'm sorry,' I say. 'No. Nothing.'

Silence can be so noisy when it falls between two people, and one is holding a secret. It stretches taut, vibrating with risk.

I can hear the dust falling in the room. The very light is audible. Thoughts racket around my head, echoing into the nothingness between us. At the same time my own heartbeat, the pulse that normally goes unnoticed, is beating like a drum, sending an unmistakeable message into that space.

Josephine looks up from her homework and stares from me to him and then looks quickly back down at her book.

We continue as before, but everything has changed. Josephine is studying the Norse gods. Harold has the paper. I am pretending to be immersed in *Woman's Weekly* – a doctor–nurse romance that is less believable than the Norse gods' stories. We are all supposedly reading but there is no sound of a page turning. The air in the room is stretched like elastic. Ready to break. Who will it hit?

Softly, I say to Josephine, 'Why don't you get ready for bed?'

She is gone as if I've just released her from a spell.

Harold goes up to say goodnight to Josephine and takes longer than usual. Maybe he has calmed down. When he comes back downstairs, he empties the whisky bottle into his glass. He picks up the paper again, but flings it down a few minutes later.

'Off to the Royal Castle,' he says.

He'll take the V8. And after closing time, he'll roar home through Above Town, revving that engine fit to wake the dead, let alone anyone who's just fallen asleep. But there's no point telling him there's another bottle of Scotch in the larder.

I can feel his tension through the bed springs. I went up early. I was so distracted I even forgot the washing-up until I was already in bed. For once in my life, I decided, it can wait until the morning. I pretended to be asleep when he came in. He won't sleep tonight, and I should be paying him attention, but just now I can only cope with this one thing. I am focused on letting go. I am untying all the precious connections with you, wrapping up the memories for safe keeping before I cast off into the void.

Little things, like the mole on your right calf, as you climb the path ahead of me in your baggy khaki shorts. High tide one hot day in June when you ran out along the rocks to dive into deep water, still in your shorts. Shaking yourself like a dog when you came out. The sun catching the droplets, so that a rainbow exploded from your head. Picking up pebbles on a beach. Wanting to give you a special find. You shaking your head.

'They lose their magic when they're not with you.'

I started, 'It's only because they dry…'

But you put your finger on my lips. 'Best leave them on the beach,' you said.

Rain-washed laughter. Windswept words. The smell of hot bracken. Brambles laced with glistening spider's webs as I picked blackberries and you watched. Always the pulse of the surging sea in our ears.

My dreamland will evaporate. The pain will fade, except on clear nights when I will remember the Yeats and look up at that crowd of stars where Love is hiding.

Are we cowards? Afraid to be happy? Afraid to live our lives? Is it ourselves we are protecting, rather than our families?

My book slid onto the floor long ago. I bring the arm that was holding it under the blankets and nurse it back to warmth. Tomorrow is another day. Tomorrow, I will concentrate on my family, my home and my husband. Tomorrow, I'll shop for

Josephine's birthday party on Saturday. Can't believe she's twelve already. That bicycle was exactly the right present. She's just mad about it. I won't even look out for you in town. It will be a fresh start.

Susan

I found it hard to say that my best friend was dead. It was embarrassing, as if I were trying to draw attention to myself, get sympathy. It was a fact. That was all.

I found it even harder to say: "My best friend was killed." It seemed like showing off, on top of all the above.

It's a day in the summer when I know Jo and I are really friends. I often go to her house after school. Jo doesn't seem to mind pushing her bicycle and she never once laughs at me for not being able to ride one. Today she has two oranges in the saddlebag. She offers me one and I long to take it.

My mouth is dry, we have a long way to go and the sun is beating down and bouncing back up off the pavement. I put my hand out, hesitate. I nearly say that I hate oranges, but instead I hear myself say, 'I don't know how to peel it.'

I burn with shame and wait for the guffaw from Jo. She doesn't even smile. She just digs her thumb into the top of the orange and I think she's going to peel it for herself and ignore me. Zest sprays the air, juice squirts out and my mouth tingles.

'Look,' says Jo, licking her wrist. 'Once it's started like that, you just pull at the skin, like this.' She hands me the half-peeled fruit, drops the peel into her saddlebag and starts on her own orange.

We've stopped at the corner where Newcomen Road meets

Lower Street, just opposite the Harbour Bookshop. Christopher Robin works there. I thought that was exciting – to meet a person out of a book in real life. But he was disappointing. Just rather shy and embarrassed, as if he'd rather be back inside the pages of *Winnie-the-Pooh*. Anyway, there I stand, prising the last of the bobbly skin off my orange, pulling the segments apart and savouring the juice as it bursts on my tongue. It is a golden moment.

Sadly for Miss Armstrong, the school attracts more girls than boys, but numbers swell and, in the autumn term, we move from her living room to the Sea Cadet Hut near the entrance to the Naval College. So now we have a huge schoolroom. Becky has left because her father has been posted to another establishment, and several younger new girls start coming, as well as Elaine who is the same age as me and Jo.

Miss Armstrong uses her influence with all friends and acquaintances in the interests of our education. Her brother-in-law prevails upon various experts from the College to visit the Hut and show us slides of warships or cloud formations, particularly Mr Barlee with his vast knowledge of birds. We go on board a visiting submarine and have a conducted tour of the Royal Yacht *Britannia* when she anchors in the river. We attend the launch of the Cromer lightship at Philip's shipyard and correspond with the master, aptly named Mr Manship, and other members of the crew.

A few weeks into our first term in the Hut, Ginny arrives. She's a bubbly personality with curly brown hair and bright eyes who chatters and gets the giggles. She's the sort of girl who makes Miss Armstrong prefer boys. Next thing I know Jo and

Ginny have ganged up. But I thought Jo was my friend. They even have a secret language. I spend hours eavesdropping, but it seems incomprehensible. Eventually I get the hang of it. I listen long enough to carefully decode what I'm hearing, and then practise until I think I can speak it as well as them. The trick is that you have to put "rug" into every syllable of every word.

One Monday at break time I say, 'Harugallorugo. Wharugat dirugid yorugou dorugo arugat theruge werugekerugend?'

Their response is surprisingly positive. Jo says, 'Wow!', quite forgetting to say, 'Worugow', and Ginny's mouth literally falls open. They both laugh and let me join in from then on.

When I think about it in bed that night it occurs to me that Jo and Ginny weren't set on shutting me out with their "rug" language. They were just having fun. All I needed to do was make an effort. After that we often play as a threesome. If we do pair up, it's usually Ginny who gets left out, sometimes me. Jo never gets left out. She's never pushy or loud, but she's always at the centre, quietly in charge.

Miss Armstrong never misses a chance to teach us something practical – she's much better at that than teaching maths, for instance, and it's much more interesting and useful. There's the time when Ginny can't flush the lavatory. Miss Armstrong doesn't send for a plumber – it's an educational opportunity. Out we all troop to the stinky outside toilets to peer inside the rusty cistern. There's a terrible stench from what Ginny's done. There's no lid, so we have to stand on the seat. We're all giggling and trying to balance so we don't fall in. But only Miss Armstrong is tall enough to reach inside the cistern. So she gives us a running commentary about how she's reconnecting the ballcock to the lever. We all hold our noses until she steps down and pulls the chain. It works, thank goodness.

One wet break time, Bobby gives us another kind of education. He's still the only boy, so he's the only one with a willy. While Miss Armstrong is on the phone in the office, Elaine dares him to get it out to show us how it works. Ginny has brothers so she's not interested and keeps cave. Jo flushes red and turns her back on us. She busies herself with painting the cardboard model of a horse and cart she's just made. The rest of us gather round to watch. Bobby's willy is pink and squashy like blancmange, and when he squeezes it, dewdrops of pee come out of the hole at the end and make dark marks on the red concrete floor.

'Miss Armstrong's coming,' hisses Ginny.

Bobby buttons his shorts and we all pretend to be looking out of the window. Miss Armstrong calls us to the table for an English lesson, and we keep looking at the wet patch on the floor and getting the giggles. We're reading "Drake's Drum", and Miss Armstrong gets annoyed. Jo is stony-faced, and it's left to Ginny to explain that we're laughing about Drake being asleep.

Afterwards Jo tells me she saw her father in the bath once.

'It was ginormous,' she whispers. 'Scary. And he was absolutely furious with me, even though he was the one who had forgotten to lock the door.'

Bobby's wasn't at all scary, so that's a mystery.

Jo and I are forever playing "Pauline and Ronald". It's a game she invented. I'm always Ronald who has to be very bossy, while Pauline is sweet and pretty and always has Ronald's meal on the table when he comes home from work. Jo tells me I'm not fierce enough and that Ronald really has to lose his temper. Then Pauline has to calm him down and bring him a drink. It's a weird game and nothing like the other games Jo likes, which usually involve climbing.

Sometimes Jo and I go to Ginny's house after school and play Murder in the Dark with her brothers and sister. If we're lucky, Ginny's father comes home early. He joins in the game, which makes it extra terrifying. Then he pours her mum a gin and tonic and makes us all his favourite food, which is beans on toast. When you see Ginny with all her family, she doesn't seem so giggly and silly. They all laugh a lot and tease each other, and it's very noisy. I never want to go home.

After school Jo and I nearly always go to the sweet shop round the corner from the Ship in Dock. We buy bubble gum, Wrigley's Juicy Fruit or lemon sherbet. We suck and chew our way across the road and take it in turns to stand on the "rocking stone", a loose capping stone on the wall bordering Coronation Park that we regularly work even looser. After that, she cycles home and I make my lonely way up Ridge Hill to our flat in Mount Boone.

Josephine

There's something not right with Daddy tonight. Not his usual "monster mood" as Mummy calls them. She doesn't say that in front of Daddy, of course. It's our secret code. This evening it's something different.

I don't notice to begin with because I'm busy finishing the invitations for my party on Saturday. I've already had my birthday – that was on Sunday, and I got a new bike from Mummy and Daddy. It was the one I really, really wanted – a Raleigh Sports with drop handlebars. It's red and I keep going to polish it, even though it's as shiny as can be. I can't wait to show it off to my friends on Saturday. I address the envelopes and get some stamps from Mummy and then Rusty and I go down to the postbox. We run all the way there and back.

I'm supposed to be going away to school after Christmas. But I've got to take an exam first. I'll miss all my friends and Miss Armstrong and the Hut people. I couldn't believe that school when I first started. It was funny sitting round a table in someone's living room for lessons. Dandy was the best thing. If you have to learn about the Romans, it's best to do it with a dog lying on your feet. And there was that brilliant view of the river. Even so, it was much better when we moved to the Sea Cadet Hut. Mummy says I'm going to find my new school very different, but I'm sure it will be fun.

*

This evening, Daddy does all the usual things in the usual order – shutting up the hens, checking that I've fed Rusty (as if I'd forget, as if Rusty would let me forget), polishing his shoes for the morning. So I can't say why I know there's something wrong, but I've always been able to tell with him. There's one thing that's different. He's reading the newspaper, that's normal, and I'm reading about the Norse gods for homework. But when I look up he's watching over the top of the paper. His eyes slide away and he carries on reading and so do I. It happens two or three times.

Tomorrow I'll write a letter to Susan. I never know what to say now we don't see each other every day. You'd think there would be more to say, but it doesn't work like that. I hope she can come and stay in the Christmas holidays. That will be better than letters. I'll tell her about the party. Mrs H is going to make a cake and I've told Mummy I don't want any pink icing. All the girls from school are coming and that nice boy, David, from swimming, plus Ginny's and Elaine's brothers because Mummy says it would be awkward if David was the only boy. I wonder if Susan likes any boys by now. She never used to.

Susan's a funny mixture. She has this very direct look and you always know what mood she's in. But she never believes she can do anything, and she used not to speak up, even when she knew the right answer. Miss Armstrong used to tell her to be more confident, but I don't think she knows how.

I remember the first time she came to tea. It was when we were still living in the flat in Kingswear and she held on to the rail of the ferry all the way across the river. Then we went in the river and she couldn't swim. A bit boring. Fancy not being able to swim at her age! She said her mother couldn't swim because the water's too cold and her father didn't like water, in spite of being in the Navy. He played cricket instead of sailing – which was a waste of living here on the river. But anyway, after that, she got her father to take her to the baths at the Naval College. She learned to swim by being dangled into the water in a canvas sling. It sounded ghastly, but she made a joke of it. I'd learned years ago by going to Blackpool Sands with Daddy. As soon as I was doing a couple of doggy-paddles, he just walked me out until we stepped off the shingle bank into the deep water. Mummy was shocked, but it worked. I mean, I couldn't have come to any harm. Not with Daddy right there to save me.

But Susan's all right once you get to know her, even if she is a bit of a scaredy-cat. Mummy says she's just a bit sensitive.

That's useful with Daddy. Because she knows almost as quickly as I do when he's in a mood. I don't have to tell her what to do, like I do with Ginny. Daddy thinks she's all right because she loves going for a ride in *Bluebird* and sitting in the dicky seat with me. Daddy likes anyone who likes his car. And she adores Rusty. It's sad that she isn't allowed a dog.

That must be because of her mother. She curls Susan's hair and makes her wear dresses and white socks. Susan should stand up to her more. But then, I'm lucky. My mother lets me do just about anything, because she says I'm sensible. Mummy was brought up in the country and I think that makes a difference. Granny lives in town now – she moved into Petersfield when Grampa died so that she could walk to the shops. When I go to stay she takes me to London on the train, which is exciting. It's as different from Dartmouth as it could be. But when Mummy was young Granny and Grampa lived in the middle of nowhere. Mummy says she ran wild as a child and wasn't at all sensible. I can't imagine it, but it must be true, because of what Granny said.

It was one day at Sunday lunch when Granny was staying with us.

'Your mummy used to be such a harum-scarum person, Josephine – when she was young.'

Daddy looked up from carving the meat. 'We all have to grow up and calm down,' he said.

Mummy was serving the roast potatoes.

'Beautifully crisp,' said Granny. 'Sometimes I find it hard to believe, Pamela, that you've turned into such a model housewife.'

'Practice makes perfect,' said Daddy. 'Don't we have any gravy?'

Mummy went pink and hurried back to the kitchen.

There was a bit of an atmosphere, because Daddy didn't like Granny saying those things. I don't think they like each other much, and I was worried that he might get into one of his moods.

But when she came back with the gravy boat, Mummy started talking about the sailing race that Daddy won last week, and everything was all right again.

I wish Daddy didn't have to get in a mood. Sometimes it's a bit frightening. But he can't help it, because he had meningitis in the War and it means he gets terrible headaches. Mummy knows what to do to look after him, though, so he'll always be all right.

Before Becky left I used to get jealous of Susan and Becky because every Thursday they'd go up to score for the College cricket matches. They got to have cricket tea in the marquee and talk to the cadets. That was a bit of a waste because neither of them was interested in boys. They tried to smuggle me in once, but Mr Pocket stopped us at the gate. His beastly dog barked like mad. I never thought I'd dislike a dog, but his looks like a white rat on stilts. Mr Pocket said both Susan's and Becky's fathers were in the Navy, but mine wasn't, so I wasn't allowed in.

'It's not fair,' I moaned to Mummy.

But she said Mr Pocket was only doing his job. 'Anyway, how would you like it if Daddy was in the Navy and had to go to sea? You wouldn't see him for a year or more. That wouldn't be much fun, would it?'

It wouldn't be fun at all because Daddy and I do lots together. He's tried to get me interested in car engines. Then I'll know what to do if I break down. At the very least I must be able to change a wheel and replace the fan belt. So far, I've only learned to clean the spark plugs. But it's ages before I'm old enough to drive. He's also teaching me to sail, which is much more interesting.

When Daddy heard about the cricket business, he said, 'Have you ever watched a cricket match?'

Of course, I hadn't. It wasn't the game I was interested in.

'You'd be bored stiff,' he said. 'But I've got a surprise for you and I don't think this will be boring.'

He'd joined the Underwater Centre – which more than made up for me not being able to go to the cricket matches. It's only just down the road at Warfleet. Daddy was the first pupil and he was so sure I would like it that he enrolled me as well. Now we go together and I'm almost as good as Daddy at swimming underwater. The instructor says my breathing is excellent and I have promise. He told us about diving with a tank. I've decided I want to be a scuba diver when I grow up.

*

When I go up to bed Daddy says he'll read to me. That's different, too. He hasn't done that for ages. I used to love it, but I'm really too old for it now. He's brought the Norse gods with him and he sits on the end of the bed reading about Odin and Thor and Loki. It annoys me how the gods were always fooled by Loki. I'm sure I wouldn't have been and I'm bored. I really want to get on with the book I'm reading.

'You're not listening,' he says.

'Can we read my book?' I take it from under my pillow and pass it to him.

'*Lis Sails the Atlantic*,' he reads out.

'It's about a girl who sails to America with her parents in a little boat. Look, there are pictures of them. It's a true story.'

He flicks through the photographs and turns back to my bookmark. 'Crazy people,' he says. 'To put your family at risk like that.'

'You've done it lots of times, haven't you? Crossed the Atlantic?'

'In an ocean-going liner, which is a bit different. One big wave could see off a boat this size.' He smooths the pages of the book. 'But at least they'd all go together, I suppose.'

'We could do that, Daddy. In our boat. Couldn't we?'

He's staring at me as if he's not seeing me at all.

'Daddy?'

'Maybe. Yes, you're a pretty good sailor.'

'We could go to France first. To practise.'

He starts to read, but his voice has got a crack in it. It's not the same as when I read it myself and hear the different voices of Lis and her mum and dad in my head. He soon stops.

'You'd better read this yourself. Another ten minutes before

71

you put the light out. I'll come up and check.'

I read, but I can't get into to it. I'm too preoccupied, wondering what's wrong with Daddy and whether he should take one of his pills. I'll wait until he comes up and ask him. I could even start that letter to Susan.

It was only when Susan was gone that I discovered what a good friend she was. Her father got posted to the Admiralty and they moved back to their house in Hampshire. I thought I'd be happy to just go around with Ginny, who's more fun, really – and she's interested in boys, so we have more in common. But Susan was loyal and reliable. I could always tell her a secret and she'd keep it to herself, which Ginny doesn't – she went and told people at Guides which boy I liked and they were all nudging each other when I came in. It annoys me when she's giggly and she can be catty as well as scatty.

Mummy's always liked Susan and says she can come and stay, so I'm looking forward to that. It will be just like before. I'll be able to stay with her, too. She's got a big garden now, with trees to climb and a beach at the end of the road. And in her last letter, she described her new kitten, which is ginger and called Morpheus because he sleeps a lot. Mummy explained that Morpheus was the Greek god of sleep. Miss Armstrong was very impressed when I told her. She said, 'Maybe that child listened in history, after all.' I never remember Miss Armstrong teaching us about the Greeks. She's always going on about the Romans.

In the end I can't be bothered to get out of bed and fetch the writing pad from my desk, so I don't start the letter to Susan and I must have fallen asleep. Because I wake up. No, I'm woken – by a big noise. Thunder? No. I know that sound. Daddy shooting rats. No. Not in the house. I rip back the bedclothes, kick free of the sheet. Rusty? Where's Rusty? Barking. Downstairs. Must be shut in. I sprint across the landing. Light's on in Mummy and Daddy's room. A smell, like striking a match, but not. Like when Rusty lies too near the fire, but not. Rusty howling. Mummy is a dark shadow lying in bed. I rush towards her.

'Mummy!'

What's wrong with Mummy? She's had a terrible nosebleed. No, worse than that. Something awful. A pong that makes me feel sick. Reach out, but I'm grabbed from behind. Roughly. Hurting. A burglar. We've got a burglar.

'Daddy! Daddy! Help!'

Where is Daddy? Why doesn't he come? Why doesn't Mummy move?

'Mummy! Mummy!'

The burglar grunts. That sound, the familiar tone. Whiff of hair cream.

Recognition. A millisecond of relief. It's Daddy. But not Daddy as he's ever been, ever.

Knowing knifes into my tummy. Thin as a razor, certain as steel. A black knowing, as if I'd stepped off that building, the one in my postcard…the one Daddy… Hurtling down, down, trying not to believe it, trying to wake up from the nightmare.

I can't see his face. I'm clamped tight, close to his body. And he's got me round the neck, my head turned away. But I don't need to see. I know anyway. That knowing I don't want tells me there is nobody to come. Even Rusty has stopped barking. I have to manage on my own. Manage Daddy.

It really hurts. Have to get out of it. Twist and squirm and try to turn away, but the harder I struggle the harder he grips me. Ouch, my neck! Like when Ginny gives me a Chinese burn, except Ginny…

'Aargh! You're hurting! Daddy, stop!'

But then it's hurting too much to say anything. Rusty must have heard me. He's howling and scrabbling at the lounge door. I try to call him. No air. Oh, Daddy, what are you doing? And what have you done to Mummy? Oh Daddy! Oh, no. No. N… Choking, everything spinning, going black.

Susan

It was six years before Mum told me what really happened. I suppose she was obliged to, because Miss Armstrong invited me and Becky to stay for the Naval College summer ball. She'd found us partners who were making up a party. Mum must have been afraid I'd find out the truth about Jo from somebody else.

I was at boarding school by that time. Mum told me in the holidays, just before I went back. No wonder nobody ever talked about that car crash. She still didn't want to discuss the shootings. She just said, 'Thank goodness you weren't staying there.' But of course, he wouldn't have done it if I had been there. It would have been a family affair. They were very close.

I didn't know how to react. I was in shock, I suppose. I was numb. I felt somehow ashamed that I wasn't more upset. At the same time, I was afraid to be upset in case people thought I was faking it, being melodramatic. Wasn't it too long ago to be sad all over again? I found it embarrassing more than anything.

I was angry, too. I'd been cheated of the truth. I was cross with Mum for the lie, for wrapping me in cotton wool and for making me go through it all twice. She didn't even apologise. As if that lie had been perfectly normal, acceptable behaviour. If we'd still been living in Dartmouth, she wouldn't have been able to get away with it. I thought of all my friends at the Hut and how I'd been cut off from them. Before it happened they used to write to me. There had been no more letters afterwards. They must have been told not to write because I didn't know the truth. They must have thought it very odd. I felt humiliated, isolated. My role as Jo's best friend had been usurped, the friendship stolen from me. Now, of course, it was far too late to do anything about it.

I wondered what it would have been like for Jo. Mum said she wouldn't have known a thing. She would have been asleep. So maybe, for her, it was better than dying in a car crash. Mum said, 'Don't think about it.' But how could I not?

I'd always had happy memories of that time. Now they had acquired an extra dimension – a patina of preciousness.

In the holidays I'm allowed to go to play at Jo's house all day, because she has a brilliant garden with woods and a barn and chickens and Rusty, of course. It's a pretty house with fancy-shaped windows, not like any I've ever seen before. Elegant, my mother calls it. Jo's mother is easy-going. The only thing we have to look out for is her father. Sometimes we'll be having tea on the lawn when he comes home. Jo knows immediately if he's in one of his moods or has one of his migraines. If it's very bad, Jo's mother telephones my mother and asks her to fetch me early. Otherwise we know to run up to Jo's room and be quiet.

We play tiddlywinks or Jo shows me her collection of picture postcards from all over the world that her father sends when he travels abroad on business. Her favourite is one of the New York skyline – all those skyscrapers with the Empire State Building at the centre.

'Just think,' she says. 'That's the tallest building in the world! The whole world. And Daddy's been up there!'

I wonder how there's any room for the people in among all those towering buildings, but I don't say anything. The picture is pinned up on her wall in pride of place.

One day, Jo and I are lying on our backs on hay bales in the barn. We've collected the eggs for Jo's mother, who's wearing her swirly green sundress and has made us lemonade. We've played Pauline and Ronald until we got bored. We've done skipping. But it's too hot for that. Even Rusty can't be bothered to fetch a stick, and the bees sound too lazy to fly.

Jo's telling me about the bats that live in the rafters when we hear footsteps. Jo stops in mid-sentence and I feel her stiffen. Her father is in the doorway, dark like a statue against the sunlight.

'There you are, girls.'

Jo breathes out along my arm. We can't see his face, but you can tell from the voice: he's in a good mood.

'Fancy a drive in the V8? A ride in the dicky?'

He already has *Bluebird* on the drive. That's the name of Mr Kennedy's special car. She's the exact same colour as the sky, a sizzling blue, the blue of electric shocks. While Mr Kennedy takes down the hood, we climb up onto the footplate and into the dicky seat. Rusty lifts up his head from the shade of the sycamore tree as we pass. Too hot for him to ride up front today.

The wind gets under my skirt as we breeze down the hill towards Warfleet and I stuff it between my knees. It's my favourite dress, blue gingham, crisp and cool, but I still envy Jo her shorts, her white Aertex shirt and, best of all, her bare feet in sandals.

The speed is making us laugh as we fly past the grey mass of the pottery. When we climb into Newcomen Road the engine noise rockets between the high stone walls and Mr Kennedy goes parp-parp on the horn, just for fun. He leans back and flexes hairy arms away from the wheel, smiling at the dials on the dashboard.

He changes down with a roar as we pass the Junior School. Jo and I nudge each other because we went there to take the Eleven Plus, and there was a boy she liked.

Mr Kennedy parks by the ice-cream shop and buys us cornets. It's even hotter in town and the heat jumps up my skirt and into my knickers as we follow him onto the Embankment. He points to a boat making for the mouth of the river.

'That's a pretty Folkboat. Time he tacked, though.'

They both watch and sigh as the sails flap and the boat changes direction. 'Just in time,' they say in unison.

'He'd better luff up, or she's going to hit the ferry.'

I've no idea what they're talking about and keep on sucking my cornet.

We wander on towards the station and watch *The Mew* crossing the river. Mr Kennedy gets his camera out of its case and takes a photo of the two of us leaning on the rail. Then we cross over to look at the old cannon.

A lady in a flowery dress steps forward and I get a whiff of her perfume.

'Can I take the three of you together? Beside the gun? If you tell me what to press?'

The sun glints on the steel frame of Mr Kennedy's glasses as he rounds on her. 'No.'

Just that one word, and he turns away. The flowery lady's mouth drops open and stays that way, like my goldfish. Jo bites her lip.

'Gun, indeed! People are so damned ignorant!' says Mr Kennedy. 'That's enough for one day.' His voice has changed and the vein at the side of his head is like a thick worm under the skin.

The dicky seat is screaming hot. Jo squawks as she sits down and claps a hand over her mouth. I spread my skirt so that she can sit on it too. No one says a word on the way back. It's time for me to go home.

Compared with Jo's place, it's boring at our flat. When Jo comes home with me, I have to explain that we can't go into the garden because it isn't ours. It seems a waste because our landlady hardly ever uses it, except to dress up in a hat and veil to smoke the bees in the three hives down by the fence. We go and look at her hens, but we aren't allowed to collect the eggs, so that isn't any fun either. She is such a fusspot. She's convinced we'll break her precious eggs and doesn't believe how much Jo knows about hens.

Jo is polite about my goldfish, Molly, and I show her where the last one, Polly, is buried in a Zubes tin under a bush in the drive. A goldfish isn't a patch on a dog, of course, but it's better than no pet. Dad won them both at the fair on the hoopla stall and we brought them home in a bag of water. Jo says she likes the dodgems at the fair best, and I say the waltzer, and we plan to have a go on them both the next time the fair comes to town for Dartmouth Regatta.

Jo loves my den under the stairs with the window looking out to sea.

'I call it the Hold,' I say.

'Like in a ship,' she says.

I nod, although that isn't why. The name just came to me and I've never questioned it.

'Wow,' she says. 'It's like a tree house.' She sniffs the air. 'Smells of wood, too. And you can see right out to the castle and the mouth of the estuary! And all the ships in the river! I'd stay in here all the time.'

So after that we take all our games into the Hold. Except when Mum joins in, like when me and Mum teach Jo how to play mah-jong. And messy things have to happen on the kitchen table. Like when we use my set of rubber moulds to make a dog and a cat out of plaster of Paris. Jo paints her dog the same colour as Rusty. Next time she comes we'll varnish them and then she'll be able to take it home with her.

Jo never did get to finish her model because summer came and we spent our time at her place, where there was so much more to do. I ended up varnishing them both and planned to take Jo's dog with me when I went to stay with her. She was going to put it on the windowsill in her bedroom, so it could see out and watch the real Rusty in the garden. Now she's dead, she'll never have her dog ornament.

Harold

I remember clearly the first dinner we had with them. Back in March, it was. He and I knew each other from the sailing club. Crewed for each other and so on. I'd only ever known him as Jonah, a nickname that pre-dated our arrival in the town.

'Pamela, Harold, how good to see you. Come in, come in.'

I follow Pamela into the hall, where a shaft of sunlight from the landing window catches her auburn hair. She has a glow on her. Some women – Jonah's wife, for instance – are losing their lustre. It makes me proud of Pamela.

'Bunny won't be a moment. She's just checking the oven.' My friend pours us each a gin and tonic.

He's a good host, generous with the gin. No interest in cars, of course. And as poor a sailor as his nickname would suggest. Evidently, the name stuck after a series of trivial incidents when skippers had bad luck when he was crewing. Not bad luck at all, I've discovered. The man is sloppy. Careless with knots, not paying attention when coiling a rope. That sort of thing. But evidently a different story when entertaining at home. I like Bunny, too – a big-boned woman, handsome rather than pretty, I'd say. Doesn't make the best of herself. Couldn't have two more different women.

I gulp the gin and I count myself fortunate to have such good friends. It's not often that both husbands and wives match so well. I'm a lucky man. Things have worked out. Setting up the pottery was a stroke of genius. Some thought I was crazy, but I've built it into a thriving business. And I have a lovely wife, a fine house and a daughter to be proud of. All things I couldn't have dreamed of after the illness.

The doctors did their best. Got me back on my feet. Recommended a steady life, routine, a rhythm I could rely on. Pamela has given me that. Stopped fussing long ago about getting a part-time job. No need, and what would people think? That I can't support my family? This volunteering, working with a woman like Bunny – that's a different matter, a positive development.

'Harold?' Bunny has come in from the kitchen and is handing round a bowl of peanuts. 'You were miles away. A penny for them!'

'Not worth even a penny, Bunny.' But, then again, maybe they are. Stock-taking thoughts. No harm in knowing when you're happy. I take a handful of peanuts, enjoying the bite of the salt against the sharp fizz of tonic water.

Bunny is confiding her latest triumph at the butcher's, leaning in a little too close. It's a way she has, to which I have become accustomed. 'Such a helpful man,' she concludes.

Jonah is at the window with Pamela discussing the pruning of wisteria. Bunny smiles across at him and continues on her round with the nuts. Extraordinary that we now have friends who discuss cheap cuts of meat and pruning.

Odd to think I'm the same chap who used to cause a nuisance on the streets of Torquay. That was in the good old days before the war, before the illness. Down with the Jabberwock team for the Babbacombe Rally. We'd had a good night out and I was on my way back to the hotel. Wee small hours. Gunning the engine – you get a great sound in a built-up area. It echoes across the buildings. Some resident must have complained. The police sergeant was not amused, got me on a charge. Now I'm a "resident" myself. I come to dinner parties and behave myself.

I'm on good form. Find myself talking to a couple about advertising. Fellow with a little ginger moustache and a wife who's too tall for him.

'The Americans do it so much better than us British. People over here don't see the importance of building the image of a company.' I'm thinking of how my co-director teases me for driving the Humber to my office each day. I could easily walk, but I have a parking space and it needs to be filled with a prestigious car. The Super Snipe is just such a car. 'Sometimes, d'you know, people here look at me as if advertising were immoral, a dirty business?'

Moustache-man is nodding, trying to look sage, but the wife laughs. 'But doesn't craftsmanship and quality speak for itself?' she says.

'Ah, that is exactly what they say. But in order for a product to speak, you must first draw it to people's attention. So I spend a lot of time being an ambassador. Gain a lot of new custom that way. Abroad mostly.'

'Oh, so you travel. How wonderful!' says the wife. 'Where do you go?'

'America, Europe, South Africa.'

She's wide-eyed. It's so easy to impress provincial folk. I'm enjoying myself.

Moustache-man ignores his wife's enthusiasm and returns to the subject of advertising. 'Isn't it very expensive? How can you be sure of getting a return? Can you measure…?'

83

I nod. 'There are sharks out there. Have to know what you're doing—'

His eyes light up. I smell a hobby horse and cut across as he starts to interrupt.

'Have to know the difference between investing wisely and squandering a fortune.'

He takes a step back and I see Pamela's head turn sharply in my direction. Must have been too vehement.

She moves to my side and proffers the bowl she's handing round. Moustache-man helps himself and ushers his wife away. Olives stuffed with pimento – angry little red eyes staring up at me.

'You know I can't stand them.'

'Of course I know.' She gives me her concerned-nurse smile. 'I was just wondering…'

'I'm fine. Don't fuss.'

I turn away to a silver cigarette box on a side table. Our hosts are not smokers. The tobacco is probably stale. But I've left my case in another suit. Pamela forgot to remind me. I light up and inhale. Filthy. I stub it straight out, saved by Bunny calling us through to dinner.

There's only one tricky moment during the meal. The too-tall wife starts a sort of game – telling your earliest memory. Load of rubbish. Who cares? But the memories erupt. As fast as I flatten one, others appear like dummies in a shooting gallery. Pop, pop, pop. Mother's in all of them. Her face in a cloud of perfume, not-Mother in empty rooms, Mother with a stranger in bed saying, 'Not now, darling. Go away, go back to bed, Mummy's busy, there's a good boy.' I douse that one. For the amusement of the table I replace it with Father coming home from a business trip with a teddy bear bigger than me. Pamela raises an eyebrow. She knows his business ricocheted between diamonds and debt and had no room for teddy bears.

In spite of that and the stale cigarettes, I am mellow when we leave that evening. We finished with some excellent port. I told a few anecdotes after the ladies took themselves off. Got them all laughing. Traveller's tales mostly. I'm not one to boast, but no harm in a few subtle hints about our customers worldwide. Let them know what's what. That the company's a force to be reckoned with. Especially that short-arse clown with the too-tall wife. Took him down a peg or two.

We chat about the other guests as we drive home. Laugh about the tall–short couple.

'She must have had to sit down in the wedding photos,' says Pamela.

We agree that we don't want to see them again, which is a relief. Pamela is reassured because Bunny cooked quite a homely dinner. A pie, it was. My wife's a good cook but she doesn't do what she calls "cordon bleu" stuff. Hates to entertain people who do. We've found our niche.

But I suffer from that stupid game during the night – it's reminded me of a true memory of Father that I prefer to forget. Wake up in a sweat from a nightmare. Falling into an abyss. It's a dream that's recurred ever since the event.

Father says he has a surprise for me. We're staying with friends on their country estate. We climb up through a bluebell wood. I wish we could stop and pick some for Mother, but Father would call me a mummy's boy. He forges ahead. When I catch up he's pointing, with a grin of triumph, at the start of a bridge. It's a thing like a hammock made of string slung across a sudden break in the woods. I look down at the bright ribbon of a river far below. Too far away to hear the water. On the other side of the ravine I can see the path continuing into trees beyond the bridge.

'See what a fun bridge this is!' Father steps onto it and it sways violently from side to side.

'The trick is to keep moving,' he shouts back at me. 'Right foot, left hand, left foot, right hand. Keep up the rhythm. You come on behind me, like this.'

I grip the rope sides with both hands.

He sets off at a brisk pace until he gets to the middle. The bridge has dipped almost into a V shape. He turns back to me.

'Come on! What are you waiting for?'

I'm waiting for the world to stop spinning. He turns a little too far towards me and to the right. The whole structure lurches. For a moment I think it will turn inside out and vomit him into the valley. No such luck. I venture forward a step or two and my knees give way. Maybe I could crawl. But Father is over at the other side now. He starts barking at me across the divide.

'Come on! What sort of lily-livered son have I got?

'Get moving!

'You're creeping like a girl!'

He's baring his teeth as if he would like to chew me into small pieces.

I've covered about a quarter of the distance between us when the hot piss starts running down my leg into my sock. If I ever do get to the other side, there will be a dark patch on my shorts for Father to mock. Cautiously, I move my right hand across to join my left and carefully twist my body so that I have my back to Father's taunts.

'Taking the coward's way out?' I hear as I drop to my knees.

The bridge starts to judder sickeningly. Father must be shaking it. I'm wriggling on my belly by the time I reach the path. I pick myself up and run for my life.

It's been there ever since, the abyss: it was there in the echo of an empty apartment after school; distant voices shouting in the void of night. When I met Pamela, she pulled me back from it. She didn't just steer me away from the edge. She removed the abyss completely. It was as if I was speeding along a mountain road – sheer drop on one side, total concentration, lightning gear changes to take the bends, one false move and you're off the road and over – and I glanced to that side, where I expected a void, and, instead, there was a sturdy fence, a green valley. That's how it was with her.

She replaced the abyss with rolling hills, firm ground underfoot. There's been the odd gully, a crevasse or two. Nothing she couldn't pull me out of. Never again the abyss.

The meningitis doesn't help, of course. It still lurks in my brain like a dragon in its den. The meninges. Used to think of them like a nest of newborns, reptilian, raw and helpless, screaming for attention. Some fever-induced fantasy. Now there's just one dragon – mostly dormant. Occasionally he wakes and fills my head with fire breath – burns the backs of my eyes, thunders into a migraine. Pamela can deal with all that. And when my red rages come on, she knows exactly what to do.

If I get restless, I take out the V8. Josephine enjoys that. She and that friend of hers love sitting in the dicky seat. We won't have another child. We're pals, Josephine and I. It's more like having a son. She makes friends easily and she's got Rusty.

I wasn't at all sure about having an animal, but Josephine and that dog are inseparable. He's part of the family now. A wise old chap.

After that first supper party we see Bunny and Jonah quite often as a foursome – meals at each other's houses, picnics up the river on the boat, a weekend sail to Salcombe and so on. All very pleasant.

Then comes that other evening. When the scales fall from my eyes. When I understand. What a fool I've been! What danger we are in.

It's just one telltale scene that lodges in my brain.

Bunny is grabbing my arm. 'Come on, people. Time to eat. My scatty husband has obviously forgotten to open the wine.' She speaks affectionately, shaking her head. 'Harold, would you be so kind?'

I look back as I leave the room, thinking to tease my good friend for this neglect of his hosting duties. He is crossing the room, gesturing for Pamela to walk ahead of him. She is looking up at him, still speaking. He is not even touching her. She is not even smiling. But an energy passes between them. Like an electric current, like sparks across plugs. Is it a trick of the light? Am I imagining it? Not according to the pain that knifes through my temple, the left side, just above the eye. I touch my hand to the place.

'Not one of your heads?' Pamela is instantly beside me, solicitous.

'No, it's nothing,' I say.

That is all. All I need.

We take our places at the table and the conversation turns

to education. Bunny was once a teacher.

'So Josephine's through the Eleven Plus,' she says. 'You must be relieved. It's a quirky kind of test.'

Pamela nods. 'That's what she said. Nothing like she was expecting. But, luckily, she made it. She's dead set on the grammar school. We've been fortunate so far with Miss Armstrong, but Josephine's going to have a shock when she gets to a conventional school. It'll be so different.'

'Let's hope she gets some decent teachers,' says Jonah.

As if it's any business of his.

'My brother teaches at a grammar in Hampshire,' he continues. 'Says the staff are all unhinged. After-effects of the war. All they care about is getting down the pub in the lunch hour. Good for nothing in the afternoon sessions.'

'What about your brother?' asks Pamela.

'He feels a bit out of it I think. He missed the war. Too young. He compensates by being rather militaristic—'

Bunny interrupts. 'Rather militaristic? Understatement of the year, dear.'

'Well, maybe.' He laughs. 'Bunny doesn't approve. He takes the boys on the ranges, you see. Teaches them shooting.'

'So that they can shoot the unsatisfactory staff?' I surprise myself with this remark and Pamela looks up, startled.

Bunny laughs, sounding a little uncertain.

'Useful skill to have. Doesn't have to be military,' I say, attempting to make amends. 'I keep it up, myself. Target practice on the rats in the barn.'

'Oh, you keep a gun then?'

'A shotgun, yes. Have to keep down the vermin. Don't we, darling?'

Is it my imagination, or does Jonah not want to meet my eye as I say that?

Pamela mutters something about the rats eating the chicken feed and me keeping everything under control. Then she turns the conversation by asking Bunny what they are doing for Christmas.

'My dear, I don't like to give it a thought until at least November. But, come to think of it, I think it's our turn to have my sister here. What about you?'

'Oh, my mother always comes. She's on her own, as you know, and Josephine adores her. They love to go off up the fields and come back laden with holly and ivy. Spend hours festooning the house.' She smiles happily round the table and meets Jonah's eye for a moment longer than necessary.

'Brings in no end of spiders and beetles,' I say.

Everybody laughs.

I've redeemed myself, put them off the scent. I force myself to eat and be merry, but I don't taste a thing and we do not stay late.

They think they are invisible. Like wearing a magic cloak. But they're careless. They've put it on inside out.

Next morning I wake with a hangover. Not surprising. But nothing to what hits me when I remember. That exchange between her and Jonah. I have a new view of my wife's radiance. I always thought she was different. The only woman in the world I could trust. The dragon stretches and jars the pain in my head. In the bathroom I mix an Alka-Seltzer, gulp it down. The clean fizz lifts my mood. Maybe it was nothing, I tell my reflection as I shave. Imagination? Jealousy? Always inclined that way. Always afraid. The dragon bares its teeth.

'Marry a plain woman, Harold. The pretty ones aren't to be trusted.'

About the only advice Father ever gave me. He was talking about Mother, of course. All those uncles who visited when he was away on business. All those nights she left me alone in the house when I was a kid. Not that he was any saint. About as reliable around women as he was with money. You learn these things about your parents. Can take years. Because you don't want to know. But in the end you have to accept it.

I pat my face dry. At least I look nothing like him. He got jowly, put on weight. Too much of the good life at other people's expense. Went to seed. I've always aimed to be as unlike him as possible. Honest in business. Shrewd, yes, driving a hard bargain. But scrupulous. Not to be a stranger to my child. Faithful to my wife. Not difficult. Never met anyone to match her. So what have I done to deserve this? She asked for the hammering I gave her last night. And it certainly made me feel better.

In my dressing room I select a weekend shirt and turn sideways to the mirror. I've kept in shape. No flab. Not bad-looking. Pamela bewitched my father, of course. Too pretty for a wife, he said. I was determined to prove him wrong. I was so sure. The dragon growls and I see Father smiling his mocking smile at me from the hellfire where he must surely be.

It's Sunday and Pamela cooks bacon and eggs – a proper breakfast with fried bread and grilled tomatoes. We sit over coffee with the papers until she clears away and starts preparing for the Sunday roast. I go off to wash the cars and tinker with the V8. Josephine's up in the woods with Rusty. All's right with the world. I put that look to one side.

But early on Monday the dragon roars. When I come

downstairs, Pamela's just come in from walking the dog. She has that heightened look that I always took to be the effect of fresh air on her pale skin. Or is it a brightness in her eyes? A different energy in the way she moves?

'Little Dartmouth, was it?' I ask.

'Yes.'

'Meet anyone?'

There it is. A split-second's hesitation.

'No. Not a soul.'

She's at the sink, filling the kettle, so I can't see her face. I wait until she turns.

'I thought Jonah went running up there? Don't you ever bump into him?'

'Jonah? Oh. Yes, occasionally. Once or twice.' She looks up, meets my gaze. 'Not this morning.'

She sets the kettle on the Aga – a clumsy movement. There's a splash from the spout and beads of water sizzle like mercury across the hotplate. That's when the dragon roars. I see it. Clear as day. A shiver of fear at the back of her eyes. I am not imagining that.

That morning Miss Thornber, my latest secretary, can get nothing right. She is aware of my condition. Knows when to lower the blind in my office against the sun; when to bring a weak tea with no milk; when to close my door and screen calls. Normally she is efficient and thorough. At midday, in exasperation, I cancel a lunch meeting and head out to Torcross. Driving the Slapton line in the Humber is a totally different experience from roaring down it in the V8. The Ford would reach its top speed quickly and hold it, vibrating like hell. The Super Snipe is altogether more dignified: elegantly gathers momentum in a smooth crescendo, and that needle keeps moving round the clock. The stretch of road isn't long enough for her to reach her full potential. The village looms and I have to decelerate abruptly and change down to take the bend. I see a raised fist in my rear-view mirror, but I'm already past the butcher's and the chapel and snaking away up the hill.

The roaring of the dragon is appeased by the power of the car and the skill of manoeuvring her. My brain is racing in tune with the engine, scanning past events when Pamela and the man I counted as my friend were in the same room. What have I failed to notice? How long has this been going on? Can I be sure?

By the time I reach Chillington I'm convinced: the answer to the last question is yes. Now there are decisions to make. How should I act? Who should I confront first?

In Frogmore I hear a police siren behind me and pull over to let the cop car pass. But it overtakes, waves me down and pulls in ahead of me. A Wolseley, the good old 6/80, beautifully polished. I wind down the window. The driver takes his time, adjusting his cap and walking back to lean in uncomfortably close. Checking my breath, no doubt.

'I'm sorry, sir, to delay you when you are clearly in a very great hurry. Can you tell me how fast you were driving, sir?'

It's a thirty mph limit through the village, of course, and I must have been doing at least fifty.

'Thirty-five? Forty?'

The officer smiles indulgently. 'Would it surprise you to know that I was having to do forty-five to keep up with you? Fifty on the straight.' The smile vanishes.

I remember that police sergeant way back when in Torquay. I was a cheeky bastard in those days, and where did that get me? Up in court, a fine, endorsement on my licence. I must be contrite.

'Oh, dear. An oversight, I'm afraid.'

'Quite a considerable oversight, if I may say so, sir.'

'The problem is, officer, I've been having a spot of bother with the carburettor. I'm on something of a test drive. And round here it's difficult to find somewhere to let her get up a head of steam.'

'In a village, sir? With pedestrians going about their legitimate business? Expecting to get home in one piece, sir?'

I put on a rueful expression. 'It won't happen again, I assure you. I was busy listening to the engine.'

A flicker of interest. Then the professional mask shuts it down.

'Was that also the case in Torcross, sir? Where a member of the public was moved to alert the police? Unfortunately for you, we happened to be at the hotel, attending on another matter.'

'I do apologise.' What bastard's got it in for me in Torcross, I wonder?

'May I trouble you for your licence, sir?'

'Of course.' I pull out my wallet. 'As a matter of interest, officer, what top speed do you get out of the 6/80?'

His eyebrows lift as he opens my licence and examines it. Maybe he recognises the name.

'All in order, sir.' He hands it back through the window. 'The Wolseley, sir?'

He knows exactly what I'm doing, but he can't resist. Within seconds we are comparing notes. He's as interested to see under the Humber's bonnet as I am to check out the Wolseley.

'So this, sir, is the six-cylinder version. No wonder you get such a turn of speed.'

When it comes to top speeds, the Humber knocks spots off the Wolseley and he knows it.

'Not that I've ever tested it, of course, officer.'

He even laughs at that and goes on about the superior road-holding capability of the Wolseley. In the end, he lets me off with a caution. If only all problems were so easily solved. I make a circuit through Kingsbridge and return to Dartmouth on the main road to avoid the temptation of the Slapton line. As I drive, I start the problem-solving process.

The abyss is back. Maybe it was always present, on the periphery. Now it's right there, centre field. I suppose you could say it's my friend. Certainly a familiar. As a young man I pandered to it: I sought out activities involving risk, danger – where feeling fear was legitimate. That way, I could avoid noticing that being fearful was my normal state of being. Speed. Height. Challenge. Anything for that adrenalin rush. No inherent danger in flying or racing, of course. Not if you're skilled and meticulous. Which I certainly was. But I was also a daredevil. To appease the abyss.

It all changed after the illness. The rallying was over. I was surprised to find I didn't crave it any more. Saw them socially, parties and so on, and I wasn't too bothered. Anyway, it's a young man's game. Business responsibilities, family took over.

I gave her everything – a pretty house, a pretty garden, pretty clothes. But it's not enough for her. I thought she was satisfied. It kept me sane. But now everything's changed again. I see I'm a man in a cage with the prettiest jailer. She doesn't look at me any more. She doesn't touch me when she passes like she used to. She walks past me, looks past me, talks to the air, not to me. I notice everything now.

No one can help me. Too close to the edge. The road collapsed straight ahead – tarmac erupting in craters, fence cascading out of sight, cat's eyes veering over the edge. The wheel judders under my hands as I slam on the brakes. My nostrils burn with the smell of rubber. Not yet. Reverse away. I don't intend to go blindly over that edge. A strategy is required. I want it to be clear that I had their best interests at heart.

This time the dragon is properly awake – not just stirring for a yawn and a shift of position. He's stretching his leathery legs and flexing his muscles. He's dragging me towards the abyss. And he's holding his fire. I sense the tension. The gathering and conserving of all that power. He will be invincible.

The plan takes shape quickly after that drive to Kingsbridge and in the following week. Every night I lie awake in the dark all through the small hours, shaping my strategy, going over and over every detail.

This is the time. This is the day. I can't wait any longer. I cannot risk a scandal. The plan is in place. It's all worked out. I've thought of everything.

We stop off at the pub for a couple of drinks. She smiles across at me as I stand at the bar. 'The usual, darling?' I ask and she nods. I chat to the landlady while she draws my pint and Pamela's half. All as usual.

We chat of this and that, the trivia of our day.

'Will you have the other half?' I ask when I've drained my pint.

Pamela checks her watch. 'No – we'll be late picking her up.'

It's time to collect Josephine from her swimming club.

I raise a hand to the landlady and open the door for my wife, as I always do. I put my hand in the small of her back as we walk out to the car. The warmth of her comes through her coat, hitting my palm. I watch the tendrils of coppery hair that curl over her collar and resist the urge to stroke her neck.

I've thought of alternatives. Driving myself into Slapton Ley, for instance. That would serve Pamela right. But it would leave her free. So that wouldn't do. What if I only killed Pamela? I'd be hanged. And Josephine would be alone in the world. What if I killed him? Everyone would know I was a cuckold, a figure of fun. Josephine would have her mother. But the child would be the victim of a public disgrace. A double disgrace. There will be no disgrace. No scandal. There is only one solution that covers all these problems: one happy family, followed by no family.

It's the only way. The alternative would be much worse. Worse for all concerned. I will not have our family destroyed publicly. We belong together and we will go together, privately, at home. I am going to save the day. She will have to go first. It is only fitting. Besides being practical.

At home, we have our meal, settle in the lounge. Josephine is doing her homework. I read the paper, taking nothing in.

When Josephine goes to bed I go up and read to her. Haven't done that in a while. But in the end I can't bear to look at her. Kissing my daughter goodnight is agony. After that I can't stand the tension. The dragon is restless. So I take off to the Royal Castle for a steadying drink or two.

When I get home I park the car in the usual place. Prepare for bed as usual. Teeth, pyjamas. Look in, as usual, on Josephine, who is asleep. When I get into bed, Pamela is also asleep, or pretending to sleep. Switch off the lamp on my side, as usual. Don't take my pill, but lie there, waiting. Stare into the darkness, going over and over the details in my mind.

When I get up Pamela stirs, but she'll take no further notice. It's common enough for me to be up half the night. I wait on the landing until her breathing returns to normal.

I call Rusty softly. He appears from Josephine's bedroom and shambles after me down the stairs, wagging his tail. This is a familiar night-time routine, where he keeps me company and gets a biscuit. I walk round the sitting room, fingering familiar objects: the smooth red lacquer of the box she keeps stamps in, the brass ashtray, the heavy glass paperweight Josephine gave me last Christmas. The silver-framed photograph of our wedding brings tears to my eyes, and I grab it to smash it onto the stone hearth. But that might wake somebody. I sit and take Rusty's head in my hands, burying my face in his rough fur to still the red rage rising inside me. "Best dog," I tell him and go to fetch his reward. While he crunches into it, I shut the door on him.

In my study everything is in order. All the papers the solicitor will need are filed neatly. Everything clearly labelled. I thought about writing a letter to her mother. But what would I say? I'm so sorry for killing your daughter and your granddaughter? Hardly. And I'm certainly not going to tell her why. That would be to go public. The police would get hold of it, it might be read out at the inquest. Perish the thought. Her mother never liked me. Never wanted me around. Wanted them to herself. So, there is no letter. Cartridges in the desk drawer.

They will say, what's the phrase? 'While the balance of his mind was disturbed.' That's what they'll say at the inquest. But nothing here is disturbed. My mind is in equilibrium.

I kick off my slippers and load the gun. I run my hands over it and set off up the stairs. The light from the landing is insufficient, so I turn on the overhead light in our bedroom.

She's lying like a child. My beloved. A fierce sweat pricks the length of my spine as I cock the gun and position it. I say her name. I want her to see me. I want her to know. But I mustn't give her time to move. I push the muzzle against her temple. She opens her eyes, focuses, the pupils dilate and I press the trigger.

I screw my eyes shut and turn away, stepping back behind the door. Only just in time. Josephine is there in seconds, running towards the bed. Was she already awake?

This means I must follow Plan B. I had hoped to get to Josephine before she woke, so that she would know nothing. Breaks my heart that she will have to suffer.

Josephine is screaming. The dog is howling and hurling himself against the door downstairs. I steel myself to act calmly.

I let the gun fall, step forward and get my arm round Josephine's neck, gripping her tight with my elbow. She twists and struggles. She's strong, my girl. But I am stronger.

How can I do this? How can I not do this? We three belong to each other. To each other, and to nobody else. Oh, I've already seen you with face powder, watching boys, making big eyes. I am doing this because I love you. Know that. I love you. I now have both hands round her neck, pressing on the larynx to compress the airway. Her struggles become more violent. I have to cause her to pass out before she twists round far enough to look at me. I fail in that. The terror, the horror in her eyes is not something I could live with. But living is not what I plan to do.

In seconds she goes limp and I let her drop to the floor. Pick up the gun and, when it's well-positioned against her skull, I press it home and squeeze the trigger.

When I open the sitting room door, Rusty rushes past me, thundering up the stairs. I can hear him whimpering as I reload the gun. Step three, I tell myself, returning to the bedroom to dispatch the old fellow. I shut the door on the scene.

Silence at last. Solitude. And one cartridge left.

Downstairs, I slide bare feet into the brogues I polished earlier and tie the laces. I'm trembling all over, shivering with cold. Could do with my dressing gown, but I'm not going back upstairs. Pour a whisky, switch on the electric fire, light a cigarette.

I settle in my chair with the gun beside me and sit, sipping the Scotch and smoking until the shaking subsides. There's plenty of time, and I need a steady hand. The orange bar of the fire is giving out heat and the Scotch is warming me from the inside.

One last smoke. I relax and listen to the silence of the house. Everything has gone according to plan. I am used to planning. I'm used to anticipating the consequences of my actions, so that is no surprise. But at this point, it is impossible to anticipate further. My mind refuses to imagine nothingness. Instead it shows me movies of myself driving down the road to the pottery in the morning, parking the car in the space marked "Director". It angers me that scenes I have no wish to see – pictures of her with him – keep recreating themselves, while my mind refuses to present me with the peace of non-existence. I can picture my life going on. At the same time I am certain that it is over. A sign that my mind is in equilibrium.

The dragon is at peace. We are at the bottom of the abyss. The abyss is, after all, my friend.

I stub out the second cigarette and drain the glass. I position the muzzle carefully.

Susan

When I discovered how it really happened, saying that Jo was killed didn't do it justice. But I couldn't say that she was murdered. I couldn't get the words out. Maybe I was in denial. Maybe it was because the truth of the tragedy kept shifting. After all, I'd had to undo six years of believing in the car crash. It made me feel odd in my stomach. There was shame involved and, even more strangely, pride. And on top of that, shame at feeling pride. Why pride? I could gloss over it by saying I was proud to have known such a special person for her short life. Rubbish! It was more like having a juicy story to tell, which would make me a more interesting person by association. But the moment I had that thought, I was overcome with shame and embarrassment. Forget I ever thought it.

I tried telling my friend at boarding school, but maybe all those doubts meant I wasn't very convincing. I'm sure she thought I was making it up, so I didn't mention it again. But there was no doubt about Jo being a special person: mad about her dog and the chickens, one minute going on about her underwater swimming and the diving school, the next dolling herself up for some boy, and all with that quiet poise and composure.

During my last term at Miss Armstrong's Jo gets interested in boys. All of a sudden she comes to school smelling of scent and with powder on her face, which, to me, is the height of sophistication. To begin with, she doesn't seem like her usual self. But I get used to it. She isn't really any different. After school she'll stop her bike at the sweet shop as usual, but instead of buying sweets, she'll start combing her hair, applying the powder and telling me who she hopes to meet.

We're coming out of school one Monday in January. I've missed Jo's Christmas party because we had to visit my grandmother for the weekend. I was very fed up, so Jo's telling me all about it.

'I meant to save you some cake – chocolate, it was. But it all went.'

I don't care about that as I'm not keen on chocolate cake. Too sickly.

'I tell you something,' says Jo. 'Boys.'

'What?'

'Boys. They're different.'

I groan, thinking of Bobby and his willy.

Jo laughs. 'No, not like that. They *smell* different.'

'Cheesy feet?' I'm thinking of my dad when he takes off his cricket boots.

'No, silly. We were playing sardines and I hid in my wardrobe. And this boy came in. It was dark of course, but I knew immediately it was a boy.'

'What did he smell of?'

'I can't describe it.'

'Maybe it's the stuff they put on their spots.' I unwrap my Juicy Fruit and slide the strip between my teeth.

'He hasn't got spots.'

'Who was it?'

'Colin. He lives near me. You wouldn't know him.'

I have a sense of Jo spinning away from me, knowing things I don't. 'Did he "do" anything?'

'No, silly. It was sardines, so we were squashed together, 'specially when the others came and found us.' She hesitates. 'I almost wished I hadn't chosen that place to hide. I'd hidden in there before – and it was safe – kind of private. Like your Hold – you know how it holds you?'

I haven't thought of that before. Maybe that is why I call my place under the stairs the Hold – because it holds me. It's so obvious now she's said that. I remember how much she liked my Hold and I'm reassured – she understands and it's something we share.

'So it was like that for me in my wardrobe – a place to go and think – and as soon as the door opened and he came in, I realised it would never be quite the same again.'

'So what was the smell?'

Jo screws up her nose, sniffing. 'Sort of like ironing. And pencils. And something else.' She closes her eyes, then opens them wide. 'I know! Metal. Like when you've been playing jacks and you've been holding them in your hand.' She sniffs her open palm and shrugs. 'Anyway, I just thought I'd tell you.'

The revelation is disappointing, just like Bobby and his willy. Why is Jo so taken up with it?

I have to ask. 'Is he your boyfriend?'

'No, silly. It was only sardines. I hardly see him except in the summer when there's sailing. He goes away to school. Who wants a stupid boyfriend, anyway?'

Jo chews intently and blows a particularly big, pink bubble. We both watch as it balloons, growing paler and more translucent until it bursts into sticky shreds.

'Bobby doesn't smell like that, does he?'

Jo giggles. 'No! Bobby smells of boat – engine oil and fried bacon. And farts. Pouf!' She makes a face. 'Anyway, he doesn't count. He's only a kid.'

She takes her powder compact out of her saddlebag and I get a whiff of peachy velvet to replace the sickly pong of the bubble gum. As she pats away with the powder puff, her freckles turn from lively and brown to pale and mysterious. It reminds me of when Mum wore her hat with the veil to a wedding in the summer.

I walk home wondering about all these things. What exactly is the not-so-subtle difference between Bobby and Colin? Why does fading her freckles to beige make Jo look so grown up? And why does she bother if she doesn't want a boyfriend? But the big question is, will she still want to be friends?

We left Dartmouth when Dad got a posting to the Admiralty. I missed Jo and was sad to think she'd have another best friend. But we still wrote letters and I was going to go and stay with her one day, except I never would now, because she was dead.

I received a parcel a few weeks after Jo died for the first time. I mean, of course, after Miss Armstrong's phone call, after I'd been told about the mythical car crash. But it is true that receiving the news in instalments, as it were, gave me the illusion that she died twice, three times, even. Once when I was eleven, once when I was seventeen and once when I was forty. I suppose it was because I had three pictures in my mind. The first was of a wreck of a car crash. The second was of Jo sleeping peacefully and never waking up. The third was anything but peaceful.

The parcel was from Jo's grandmother. I'd met her once

when she was staying with them. It contained a shoebox and inside was a book called *Lis Sails the Atlantic*, Jo's red tartan pencil case and a Spanish doll from her collection of dolls in national dress. Her father always brought her one back whenever he travelled abroad to a new country. I put the doll in a box and rarely looked at it.

The book looked dull. A plain hardback with nothing but a compass rose on the linen cover. But I did read it – a true adventure of a girl and her parents sailing to America in a small boat. I envied her for being Scandinavian and different and not going to school for a year, but that was all. I only kept the book because Jo had written her name in the front. But, that pencil case of hers – I'd always liked it and I used it until it fell apart.

A second parcel arrived the following year, from Miss Armstrong. The Hut School was closing and Miss Armstrong was off to teach in a boys' prep school. She sent me the Hut logbook – the journal of the "Britannia Crew". The flyleaf records an obligation to contribute one penny a week to the Mission to Seamen during the summer holidays and states that one shilling and eleven pence halfpenny was collected in this way in 1954.

The logbook reported the movements of ships in the river. Frequent visitors were HMS *Redpoll*, frigate; *Similarity*, collier; HMS *Starling*, frigate; and *Vestal*, Trinity House vessel. It was reported that *The Mew*, the railway ferry, resigned after forty-six years because her keel had rotted. The Royal Yacht, HMY *Britannia*, visited in July. The collier *Similarity* alternated with her sister ships, *Singularity, Security, Amenity, Speciality* and *Continuity*, all of them painted lemon yellow. A whole section covered the Torbay to Lisbon Tall Ships race of 1956, with pages of sketches and photographs of these magnificent vessels in full sail.

Miss Armstrong sent me a photograph for Christmas that year. It was taken in the summer after I left, a few months before the tragedy. It's in black and white, of course, an enlargement, and shows the school sitting on the grass outside the Hut with Coronation Park in the background. Miss Armstrong must have had a piece of glass cut specially and she'd framed it very neatly with grey passepartout.

Miss Armstrong was in the middle flanked by the younger children and Ginny. Jo was the only one standing and she had her hands round the point of Miss Armstrong's crazy straw sun hat. Miss Armstrong was wearing a fixed smile, Ginny was grinning, giggling probably. Of the other children, one was leaning towards the camera in a film star pose. Typical, I thought. Ginny's sister was looking defiant, cross-legged with her knees sticking up, but was smiling in spite of herself. A small boy I didn't know was crouched, ready to leap up and run off. So much tension. Only Jo was poised and serene. She was smiling slightly, a quiet, presiding presence.

Many years later, when I allowed myself to think about it, I realised it was highly unlikely that Jo was asleep when she was killed. Her father would have been in a worse mood than usual. Jo was always so attuned to his moods. She would have been anxious. She might have stayed awake listening. Maybe there was a row going on downstairs.

And apart from all that, there were the practicalities, the logistics to consider. Her father probably wouldn't have killed her first. Surely the sensible strategy would be to shoot the adult first. Besides which, surely it was his wife he *wanted* to kill, making the death of my friend collateral damage. So Jo would have been woken by the first shot.

It was then I ordered the newspapers from the British Library, the ones I hadn't been allowed to read. That's when I found out what really happened. It was as I suspected. Jo was not asleep.

The local press was restrained, respectful. But the national newspapers went for sensation. I found one headline particularly chilling: "Tragedy in Birthday House". The item described how Jo had apparently "danced" to the postbox with her birthday party invitations. How dare they! How could they know? It seemed "a neighbour" had supplied the information. I shuddered to think of the interview.

I became obsessed with other similar cases. I cut them out of the newspaper. It really wasn't that uncommon. I read the accounts closely, trying to understand what possesses a man to kill his whole family and then commit suicide. For they all did seem to be husbands and fathers. Why did my friend have to die? Why was she murdered? Murdered by the father who adored her?

Much later I fell to wondering about how the survivors had coped. How did they explain it? How did they begin to make sense of such an event? And how did they manage to carry on with their lives?

Jonah

'Have you heard?'

'Dreadful, isn't it? Those poor people!'

'Alec saw the ambulance.'

'The whole family, yes.'

'Poor Mrs Harrison, what a thing to find!'

'It was her daughter phoned my Jennifer.'

There's a lot of gossip going on as I make my way through the town. But I'm miles away, thinking about Pamela, who wasn't walking her usual route with Rusty this morning. She must have meant what she said yesterday. No more meetings on our own. I agreed, of course. I meant it, too. It was the only sensible way. But this morning, sensible strikes me as bleak and foolish. You only have one life.

I've wasted the morning shuffling paper. Listless. Preoccupied. The only thing that got me moving was the possibility that I might encounter Pamela if I went to the bank. She often went shopping at this time. And I did need some cash.

It's my turn at the counter. Mrs Clarkson, usually chatty, takes my cheque with a brief nod.

'How would you like the money?' she asks.

'Five ones, the rest tens,' I reply.

She counts the notes and pushes them across to me without once making eye contact. Maybe her husband is ill again. On another day I would enquire after him, but I'm impatient to get outside to that possible chance encounter.

I pass three ladies outside the bank.

'That Josephine. Such a sweet girl. I just can't believe it.'

My stomach contracts. I want to grab the speaker and ask her what they are talking about. But she sees me and turns her back.

I become aware that the town is in ferment. It reminds me of the time I sat on an ants' nest. At first I noticed one or two ants, then quite a lot of ants, until I realised that the whole patch of grass was a seething mass of the creatures invading every part of my clothing. It isn't idle chatter I'm hearing as I walk back to the office. There are no casual acknowledgements. No "All right, me 'andsome?" and "Cheerio" greetings. Knots of people are gathered along the Boat Float. The whole staff of Cundell's seems to have come out onto the pavement. People are grabbing each other as they meet. They are talking and listening with unaccustomed intensity, wide-eyed, open-mouthed.

I hear repeated phrases: "the whole family", "'the pottery", "that poor child". I need to know, but I dare not ask.

My secretary is on the phone when I walk into the front office. She sees me and her hand flies to her mouth as she replaces the receiver on its cradle.

'Anything wrong?' I ask.

'No, nothing. Nothing at all.' She looks flustered.

'There seems to be something going on—' I begin.

'Your wife phoned. She said to phone her right back.'

Bunny tells me to come home immediately. 'Don't speak to anyone,' she says.

*

I'm not proud of how I'm coping with this. I'm not coping. When Bunny told me, we clung to each other. We were both shaking. It was like hearing news from another planet, an alien thing. As the day wore on, we wandered about the house, sat down, got up abruptly and paced about.

Later she says, 'I don't suppose anyone would look you in the eye.'

I look up sharply. 'Well, no.' I remember her words on the phone. 'You told me not to talk to anyone. What was that about?'

'I've known for months,' she says.

That word. "Known." It seems to suck the air out of the house. My stomach caves. There's nothing to hold onto, no straw to clutch at.

'Known what?' I say, like the idiot I feel.

'Don't give me that.' We've encountered each other in the hall and she turns away, speaking to the hatstand. 'And also, there's been a rumour going around recently. That is, according to Ann Smith, who phoned me this morning. She does tend to be accurate about these things.'

'But it wasn't—'

'So, you do admit it. There was an 'it'.'

'It wasn't—'

'I don't wish to know what it was or wasn't.'

She's been sitting it out, she says, waiting for it to fizzle. 'Affairs tend to do that,' she says.

I draw breath, shut my mouth again.

'And if it hadn't, I could have coped. I was much more concerned for Harold. But I never... How could anyone begin to imagine?'

I can't manage any more talking and I take to the spare bed

with the curtains drawn. I can't stop shivering.

Oh, Pamela, you dear sweet, lovely girl. Whatever went on last night? Between the two of you? In your house? In his head? This wasn't the end you had in mind. I was thinking it would be torture to see you only in the company of others. How lightly we use words. *This* is torture. Knowing I'll never see you again. Not knowing what you endured.

As the hours turn into days, the torture twists up steadily, notch by notch. He must have known. Did someone tell him? Did you tell him? Did he guess? He must have put two and two together and come to his own conclusions. Acted in a frenzy of jealousy. His wife and his friend betraying him. Another man appreciating his wife, trespassing on his property. Which makes it my fault. I failed you, Pamela. I had no conception of the sickness of the man.

I have a picture of the two of us like a pair of children, carefully dousing their campfire, blissfully unaware of the volcano erupting with molten lava behind them.

But then again, what if it was nothing to do with us? It could be the business. A massive failure. I spend a whole day believing that, exonerating myself. As if that – my guilt – were the more important issue. Until I notice that my lack of guilt brings no relief – it doesn't bring you back.

A week drags by. Then comes news of the inquest. No evidence of imminent bankruptcy or fraud. Harold's affairs were perfectly in order.

'You mustn't blame yourself,' says Bunny.

I can't help thinking that she blames me. Sometimes she can't look at me or be in the same room. She is very matter-of-fact about this.

*

'What on earth are you doing? Oh, no, it's *Lady Sylvia*. You're murdering *Lady Sylvia*!'

Bunny's voice filters through my rage as I make another frenzied attempt to yank out the root. I've hacked off all the branches and chopped the main stem down to a couple of feet. I grip the wood with both hands, hook my fingers into the earth to get a purchase on the roots and heave. It begins to shift, and with a final wrench it tears free, landing me on my back among the thorny cuttings. I roll away from Bunny, who is standing over me.

That morning I decided it was time to stop brooding behind closed curtains and get into the garden. What started out as a pruning exercise has somehow morphed into an act of violent mutilation. At some point I had the thought, how dare this puny rose still be alive? With every strike on the plant I inflicted a laceration on myself. Each injury brought a moment of relief. But no graze or gash could inflict enough pain.

I get to my knees and survey the carnage. Bunny's words echo back into my consciousness.

'She wasn't doing very well,' I say as I stand up.

'But she was one of my favourites. Surely—'

Then Bunny sees my face. She covers her mouth with her hand. 'Oh, my dear,' she says. 'My dear old darling.'

She leads me indoors, sits me at the kitchen table, pours me a brandy. She fetches an old flannel and towel, bathes the mud and blood off my face, dabs the scratches with TCP, produces tweezers, picks every thorn and prickle out of my hands, lays them in a fresh basin of water. It's only lukewarm and she is gentle, but every movement stings. I welcome the pain.

When she has finished she folds my hands into the soft towel. It's threadbare in places and coming unstitched along the hem. I feel profoundly grateful for its comfort and for having a wife who has kept such a towel.

Bunny tips away the water and swills the bowl. She speaks from behind me.

'You really were very much in love with her, weren't you.'

It isn't a question. Nor is it a protest. It's a very Bunny-like statement of fact. I'm overcome with admiration for my wife. The tears finally erupt. I don't know how long I sit there, burying my face in the towel. Bunny is still standing at the sink, gazing down the garden when I emerge.

'She never—' I begin.

Bunny turns to me and holds up a hand. 'No need,' she says. 'Now, you'd best go up and scrub your nails.'

When I come downstairs, the remains of *Lady Sylvia* have disappeared and Bunny is putting the wheelbarrow away. She's red-eyed when she comes back in.

'I'll make some soup,' she says.

My efforts at returning to work are no more successful than my attempt at gardening. The clerks don't know how to behave towards me. My secretary has cancelled my appointments and clients have transferred to my colleagues. I go in late and come home early for a few days. Then I give up and spend my time walking the cliffs and beaches or mooning round the house starting endless crosswords that I fail to complete.

It's several weeks after the tragedy when Bunny interrupts *The Times*' cryptic.

'Just for once, can we pretend it didn't happen—'

I cut across her. 'What? The murders?'

'Let me finish. Of course not the murders. Your relationship with Pamela, whatever it was, is what I mean. Because we need to grieve – both of us – for the loss of our *friends*. I have pain, too.'

I'm about to protest that I'm not claiming to have more pain. But actually, that is exactly what I'm claiming. She takes no notice of my intake of breath.

'Pamela and I were very close. I was very fond of her. I'd like to mourn her without thinking of her as the other woman. I don't know what you feel about Harold. He was your friend. But I was fond of him, too. He could be an awkward bastard, but I could cope with that. I always thought of him as an honest person, loyal to family. A man of integrity. And that child – she was a sweet thing, sparky and funny. I was looking forward to seeing her grow up.'

Bunny's face is suddenly shining with tears. Bunny. Weeping.

'That kid had her life before her. He had no right. That's what matters. Not whether you—' She shakes her head and glares at me. 'I'm sick of your guilt. If you think you have the monopoly on feeling guilty, then go tell Pamela's mother that it was your fault. Tell her, 'I'm sorry he chose to kill her and not me.' See how that will help.'

I frown. I can't see how this conversation is helping. It's not like Bunny.

'You could say we're all guilty. Me, for one. Why didn't I confront you? Talk to her? What was she thinking of? She knew what Harold was like. She was taking a huge risk.'

'She called it off. We weren't going to meet again.'

115

'Too little, too late. Obviously. If *I* could notice there was something going on between you, then Harold could notice. So Pamela has to take a big slice of responsibility.'

Bunny falls silent. Then she laughs, a humourless bark.

'And there we are, talking about you again, you and her. Which is what I wanted to get away from.' She takes a deep breath. 'I'll bet her mother is asking the same questions, wondering what *she* could have done for her daughter, what she didn't notice. But the point is, it was Harold who fired the gun. There are plenty of men in the world who discover – or imagine – that their wives are unfaithful, but very few of them murder their families. It was a choice he made.'

I nod, unsure of how I should respond. Bunny hardly seems to be talking to me.

'He acted according to his principles, I suppose. No shame must come on the family, betrayal of trust must be punished. Something like that?'

'A bit—' I start to respond, but Bunny ignores me.

'You could blame the doctors for not recognising the risk, not giving him adequate medication. But how could they know? He put on such a good front. Competent, charming, devoted husband and father. How could anyone guess what was going on behind all that?'

I shrug. 'Indeed.'

'You could blame his parents for bringing him up to hate women.'

'Oh, come on—'

'Oh yes, he did. That's why he and I got on so well. I have no illusions – I'm not a very feminine woman. He worshipped Pamela, but it covered a deep mistrust. I'd put money on it.'

'Sounds like you're saying, he was perfectly sane, he made a choice, but he's not to blame. That's a total contradiction.'

Bunny shook her head. 'Not a contradiction. It just is complex. Not black and white.'

'I don't see the point of all this.'

'I thought it would appeal to you. You're always analysing everything. But now I'm doing it and it makes you uncomfortable. But you're in no position to complain.'

She gave me a twisted little smile – almost of triumph. An expression I'd never seen on Bunny before. Then she was off again.

'The point I'm making is that nobody is to blame and yet everybody played a part. We all have responsibility but it's nobody's fault. If this dreadful event has taught me anything, it is that we are all connected and if we don't accept that, then we're no better than Harold.'

I pour us both a brandy. We're getting through an awful lot of it lately, but it's all I can think of by way of response. And I definitely need one.

I raise my glass. 'I think we should drink to the memory of our friends. And the good times we all had together.'

Bunny clinks her glass against mine. 'Thank you. Yes, I'll drink to that. The fact is, we shall never know what went on in that house on that night, let alone what went on in his head. Pamela was asleep, we know. Which is more than can be said for Josephine. That is what I cannot forgive. Allowing that poor child to suffer. Imagine. Your own father. No, I can't bear it.'

We are both silent. I'm seeing the special expression on Pamela's face when she spoke of her daughter, her eyes full of a kind of love-light that was quite different from the way she looked at me.

'You know something Harold told me once?' Bunny sips her brandy and carries straight on. 'He was complaining about having to get back for the babysitter – and about Pamela insisting on having one. Said Josephine was old enough to be left alone. Said his mother regularly left him alone at night, right from when he was four or five. Evidently his father was away a lot on business but his mother didn't let that cramp her style. Quite a society lady, I gather. He said – Harold said – it never did him any harm.'

'Harold told you that? He never used to talk about his family.'

'I know. I was surprised. He'd had a few, but even so. I suppose he trusted me.'

'Sounds like you two got on in the same way as me and Pamela.' Why do I say that? I don't really believe it. But for a moment, it makes me feel better. Until I get Bunny's reply.

She glares at me. 'An anecdote over the washing-up? I don't think so. Nobody was spreading rumours about us.'

We don't do Christmas. I don't know how, but Bunny gets us out of all the traditional commitments. We hibernate with corned beef hash and plenty of wine. There are none of the usual invitations for New Year celebrations, so we're obviously going to spend that alone too. On the morning of New Year's Eve, she's making a curry and I'm sitting over a coffee at the kitchen table when she makes her announcement.

'We have to leave this place. Hardly anyone wants to know us. Not in the normal way. They're either too friendly in that unctuous way with the hand on the heart or grasping your hand in both of theirs. Or they avoid me. I prefer the avoiders. You hardly poke your nose out except when most normal people are still in bed.'

'But you have friends. What about Ann—'

'Oh, yes. Ann says she still can't believe I didn't intervene. She puts her head on one side and looks at me as if I have a screw loose. And Betty says, "We don't hold your husband responsible. Of course we don't, do we, Ann?" And there they are, the two of them, a gang of two, united in being tolerant. And me on the opposite side of the table, as it happens.'

'I'm sorry, Bun.'

'And if you say sorry one more time in that "I have to humour her" voice, I'll… I'll… I don't know what I'll do.'

She throws down the oven glove and storms off upstairs.

That evening she revisits the conversation, the feeling of being ostracised.

'It will pass,' I say.

'It will not pass. Or not until I'm in my dotage. I'm not prepared to wait and see. Nor am I prepared to watch you mooning about the countryside, seeing the ghost of Pamela at every turn.'

'That's harsh. How can you be so—'

'Callous? Cruel? I hurt too, remember. I'm being practical. You don't have to come with me. I'm perfectly capable of starting a new life on my own. But I'd prefer not to give the gossip-mongers of this town the satisfaction of seeing us separate.'

Sometimes Bunny's capacity to be practical takes my breath away.

'A fresh start. That's what we need. In a place where nobody knows us. And just for the record, I hope you come too, old thing. I really would prefer it.'

I've stayed in survival mode, not giving the future any thought. But as soon as I think about it, I know Bunny is right. The move becomes our New Year resolution.

The last thing I do before we leave, early in the morning before the removal van arrives, is go to the stile – you know the one – to talk to you.

I let you down, love of my life. I should have been more vigilant. You knew there was a risk and you withdrew. Too little, too late, as Bunny said. But it staggers me, humbles me, to realise how much "us" must have meant to you, to run the risk you did. Did I say, "humbles me"? Rubbish! It makes me proud.

I've just realised I'm staring at a clump of primroses – the same primroses. It's a year almost exactly since it all started from a chance encounter on my run. Oh, my dear love.

I have such a dilemma. I cannot, cannot wish that "us" never happened. And yet, if it hadn't happened, you would still be here. I can't resolve that one.

They say you have to be able to let go of a person if you truly love them. I did let go. But did I really mean it?

The will decided. But how can the heart decide…?

That's Stephen Spender – I can sense your inner groan at yet another poet to contend with. Bunny's with you there. She says I'm "wallowing in it" when I read poetry. But the poets have a knack of putting their finger on it, expressing what I feel so much better than I can. That last morning, my heart certainly hadn't decided and there wasn't time to find out if my will would have stayed strong. I certainly never expected to have to let go so completely. I thought I was committed to you, light of my life. But not as committed as Harold. He was so committed that he committed murder and suicide rather than lose you.

What's the phrase?

The best lack all conviction

Yeats, this time. It's in that book I gave you, about halfway through. Can't remember the title. But is it *conviction*? Or *commitment*?

The best lack all conviction, while the worst
Are full of passionate intensity.

Definitely *conviction*. Which was I? The worst, I suppose, but compared with Harold, my passion and intensity were insipid. You're definitely laughing at me now. You were too practical to get caught up playing with words. Clear-eyed, living your life and making the best of the choices you'd made. Being with me was a deviation. "Us" tempted you. I truly believed I was helping, giving you an outlet, some fun. It was entirely selfish, of course. And for you it was fatal.

Bunny has been remarkable. She's supportive in a harsh sort of way. She thinks my feelings of guilt are self-indulgent. How can I not feel guilty? But then again, I could spend my time blaming myself. With "passionate intensity".

She mourns you as a friend. She won't see you as the other woman, hasn't shown any hurt or jealousy. The horror of the ending made it irrelevant, I suppose. She even said how much she cared for Harold.

I thank God you were asleep. I know that means Josephine was not – which makes Bunny incandescent with rage. I regret that – of course I do – but all my concern is for you. If I said that to Bunny she would know me for the monster I probably

121

am. It's as if all our normal emotions have been exploded into the air, and we don't know where or how they'll come to earth. Maybe they never will.

It was Bunny's idea to move. A fresh start away from the ghosts. You'd probably agree with her. But I know you will come with me. She says we'll make new friends. I can't imagine that. I just know I don't want anyone calling me Jonah ever again.

Mrs Harrison

I'm not myself. The doctor's been very good. Right from the start. And I'm better than I was since he give me the nerve pills. And the ones for sleeping. The policeman was good, too. Steady. Patient. 'Take your time, Mrs Harrison.' Very respectful. Bert was there, of course. They sent him home from work. Paid him, too, all that first week. Said it was the least they could do. Anyone would think it was our family it happened to.

Trouble was, I had such awful nightmares. Bert didn't know what to do with me. Then I got afraid to go to sleep. Days on end without a wink. I was good for nothing. So the doctor come again and gave Bert another prescription to take to the chemist. 'Keep them out the way,' he said. 'Not where any kiddies can get at them.'

Trouble is, when you sleep, you have to wake up. And then it starts all over again. What it is, it's like having wallpaper inside your head. But not wallpaper anyone would ever want on their walls. There were days when I never got out of bed. That must have flummoxed Bert. I'd burrow into the blankets and pull the eiderdown over, like we used to stack sandbags on top of the Anderson shelter in an air raid. And when I got too hot, I'd poke my nose out and just lie there, staring at the ceiling or watching the clouds go by. A lot goes on up there on the ceiling. You see the light move across it. I could cope with that.

Our Rosie came in for the first few weeks. Every day, after

she'd taken the kiddies to school. Did a bit of shopping, cooked a tea – so all Bert had to do was put it in the oven. And she'd say, "Don't upset yourself, Mum," and make a pot of tea and tell me about what the kiddies were doing and I'd see her trying to think of things to talk about that didn't lead back to that one thing we were never going to talk about. She would read me the story in *Woman's Own* and try to get me knitting again, saying, "That's a nice pattern, Mum," and mentioning that little Jennifer could do with a new jumper for Christmas. But it went right over me. I couldn't catch on to anything.

After that first couple of weeks I could see our Rosie looking at me. She didn't say anything, nor nothing. But I always could read her. "Come on, Mum. Time you pulled yourself together." That's what she was thinking.

Trouble was, that's what I kept saying to myself. But it didn't work. I'd tell meself to do things but my body wouldn't do them. "Snap out of it," I'd say. "Dust this room," I'd say. "Go on. Get on with it." Hours later I'd still be sitting there with a cloth in my hand when I'd hear Bert's key in the lock. Where had all that time gone? His face would fall as he walked through the door and found me there, same as yesterday, same as the day before.

But Rosie has her own life to lead, so I told her she need not stop any more. She still does a bit of shopping and drops in a pie when she's baking. Sometimes I manage to peel a potato. I have the wireless on most of the time. It's company. *Music While You Work* (except I don't), *Listen with Mother* (except I'm on me lonesome) and *Woman's Hour*. I like the shipping forecast best.

In the evenings Bert sighs a lot and rattles his paper. He watches me over the top of it. And me just sat there, staring at the wall. Where's his wife gone? That's what he's thinking. I can't tell him where she went. Or when she'll come back. I miss her too, I want to tell him. I'm so lonely without her. But I can't find no words. All that comes is tears. I don't cry. What it is, my eyes leak. I don't notice until Bert gets out of his chair and comes over and mops me up with his handkerchief. Gentle, he is. I wish he could fix my eyes like he put a new washer in the kitchen tap when it dripped. But he just kisses the top of my head and puts the kettle on.

Bert only got cross once. The neighbour came by with a bunch of flowers out of her garden. Michaelmas daisies, they were. A great bunch of purples and pinks looming up at me.

'Don't give me them,' I said. 'Take them away,' I said. And I clapped my hand over my mouth.

She walked straight back the way she came and slammed the door before Bert had time to see her out.

'Now look what you've done!' he said. 'Upset poor Elsie. What you want to do that for? Just a few flowers to cheer you up.'

But I wasn't hearing, only seeing those Michaelmas daisies in that border outside the back door of the house in the road I would never walk down ever again.

The mother came to see me. Mrs K's mother, I mean. Lovely woman. I'd met her a few times out there when she came to stay. I began to think, what must it be like for her? But I couldn't even get to the end of the thought. She didn't say, "Don't upset yourself," or "Time will heal," or any of those things.

She said, 'Don't even think of making tea. I expect we're both drowning in tea.'

She set a bottle of brandy on the table. 'For Christmas, if not before,' she said. 'I brought some leeks from the garden. Shame to waste them.'

And she stood at the sink and washed them and cut them up and got me to show her where the compost heap was for the trimmings.

Then she said, 'I brought you another thing. If you'd like to have it. A reminder of the good times, I thought.' She was fishing in her bag and handed me a little box.

A brooch, it was. A tiny basket of flowers done with seed pearls and tiny stones. Mrs K used to wear it a lot. It was her favourite brooch. I wanted to say it was too much. Turned out I didn't need the words that wouldn't come.

'Gold and emeralds. I know. But that's not the point. Nothing will make up for what you went through. Point is, she'd have liked you to have it. Pamela was very fond of you.' She took the brooch and pinned it on my cardigan – my old brown, lumpy cardigan.

Then she took my hand. 'The thing is, you carry a horror that should have been mine. Nothing can change that. But it should never have happened to you.'

After she'd gone, I got in that kitchen and tied on my pinny. First I washed the floor. Then I did potatoes and cooked the sausages Rosie had left on the table. Just the thing to go with those leeks. I was shaking by the time I finished. But Bert looked so pleased when he came in.

It was after that the worm started. It began with a wriggling in my head like the start of a headache as I lay in bed, gnawing through the darkness, screwing its way out of my brain, boring a passageway through the fug of the bedclothes, and still there when Rosie came and got me in the bath, not hot enough and not too long, Mum, and persuading me to a slice of bread and butter with my tea, nice and strong. And still there after she'd gone, I've got shopping to do, Mum, and following me into the cupboard under the stairs to fetch a duster and looking me in the eye in the mirror as I dusted the clock on the mantelpiece, making me forget to do anything else. And still there when I woke from a nap I never meant to have and bursting out of me when Bert came through the door as if it had been waiting for him all day.

'The nerve of the man! The nerve. How dare he?'

And Bert's eyebrows beetling up into his hair, which is still thick and only just getting a bit of grey at the sides, because he isn't used to me saying anything much at all when he comes in.

'What do you mean, love? Who—?'

'Him. Him. Who else? I mean, he's welcome to kill himself. It's his own life. But how dare he think he had the right… She was living her own life. Best she could.'

'I suppose he thought—'

'She couldn't live without him? That's what I mean. The barefaced nerve of the man.'

Bert's scratching his chin and looking at me, quiet, like. And after a while he goes out to the kitchen. He must be disappointed – no sign today of me making him any tea.

Later that evening he brings in a cup of tea and a Rich Tea for supper.

He takes hold of my hand and squeezes it. 'We can never know,' he says.

I wonder if he means we can never know what was in that man's mind, or we can never know what anyone is thinking, because I surprised him and he might surprise me if I knew what to ask, but I'm afraid to for fear of what I might find, and I think that is what goes wrong in the world and that makes me no better than that man but I'm too tired to be brave. Maybe the worm will carry on and break out a bit more of itself tomorrow and I'll try again.

Bert said, 'What about going to the carol singing?' and I surprised myself by saying yes. It was my first time out the house. There was quite a crowd round the bandstand but nobody noticed me in the dark. Bert got hot chestnuts from a stand by the fountain. They warmed my hands through my gloves, Bert's arm was round me, and the words of the carols came tumbling out my mouth automatic-like. All those voices sending the sound up to the stars. For a little while I lost meself. I forgot. Then we started on "In the Bleak Midwinter". It was Bert's favourite. I don't know why, but it brought it all back. Bert noticed me shaking and he said we'd go home. As we turned away, I heard someone say, 'Poor woman. Witnessing a thing like that, it's bound to scar you for life.'

Bert had to practically carry me home. 'Take no notice,' he said.

But I did take notice. It made me feel better, not worse. It made me feel I wasn't the fraud I was afraid I might be. I wasn't making it up.

Come the summer, Rosie comes by one day with the kiddies and a picnic.

'Come on, Mum. Do you good to get out. It's a lovely day.'
'Please, Nan!'

'Not too hot. Bit of a breeze.'

'I'll hold your hand, Nan.'

They've been plotting and I'm pleased. I want to please them. I want them to think I'm better. But it turns out they're set on walking out to the castle, kiddies looking forward to a swim in the cove.

'No,' I say. 'Not today.'

Not today. Not any day. Not ever. Never will I go that way, out there to Warfleet and past the pottery. I give them money for ice creams and turn on the wireless.

Josephine's Grandmother

I feed the hens and then I walk up the field beyond the barn and the farmyard to the edge of their well-fenced land.

In the corner of the field stands a barn. It's very different from the well-maintained buildings down in the yard. On the weather side, the slates have been replaced with a sheet of corrugated iron, now rusting and crooked where the fixings have slipped. The north-easterly rips down the valley and catches under the loose corner of metal, lifting it and slamming it down. The creak and clang of it echoes across the field, joining the clatter from the rookery in the woodland on the far side.

This is where Josephine and I used to come when she was little, bringing a picnic and playing hide-and-seek. Sometimes we were joined by the neighbours' children. When Josephine was older we came to fetch greenery to decorate the house at Christmas, peeling long tresses of ivy away from the stonework where it gripped with ant-leg tendrils. She and I dragged back armfuls to trail about the house. 'Deck the halls.' Make a wreath. Not this year. Not ever again.

The years have taken their toll. The back elevation has collapsed at the corner and the stones are heaped like a cairn, awaiting some long-forgotten labourer who might once have rebuilt the wall. Brambles have meanwhile filled the gap, invading the space that once kept hay sweet and dry all winter.

Two rooks circle overhead, banking into the gale. They

swoop in to land on the exposed beams, ungainly on bandy legs, swaggering sideways, jostling for position and cocking sharp eyes sideways towards the floor. One drops down out of sight. The other struts about. They swap over. I watch them fly up and down, feeding on leftover grain, squawking, preening and finally taking off back to their home in the tall elms.

The double doors are sagging on their hinges and a rusty chain keeps them from swinging open. They creak in the wind and every so often a gust pushes them inward, slackening and rattling the chain, until they bulge back out and stretch it taut. In out, in out, like a leaky bellows.

I step through the side door, which is jammed open on rusty hinges. Inside it smells of dust and decay. The floor is littered with the remains of hay bales, ends of binder twine and the lime from a swallows' nest wedged up into the far corner. A pile of sacks vibrates a memory and children's voices echo up to the rafters, raw, visceral. *Bags I, Feigns! One potato, two potato...you're on it!* and one clearer than the others: *ready or not, here I come!*

Turn away. Don't go there.

In spite of the damage at the back, the other walls are solid. As the light fades, a flurry of snow brings more voices on the wind: *earth stood hard as eye-on, water like a stone, in the bleak midwinter.* Flakes fill the air, sliding off the ivy, too wet to stick. A lone herring gull heading inland is barely visible and the rookery has vanished into the whiteout. *Abide with me, fast falls the eventide.* I turn and stumble back the way I came, vision blurring, as the snow turns to sleet.

I can hardly bear to go into the study. But I owe it to her. To try to understand the enigma of the person she married. On the one hand, he was addicted to speed – motor racing, flying – as if he sought to outdistance himself, to exorcise the part of himself that dealt in risk and danger. On the other hand, he set about building a solid business out of something as harmless as domestic pottery. On the one hand, charming, on the other, moody and stormy. I was never comfortable with him, but I never thought he was a bad man. There was certainly never anything to suggest he was capable of this – this thing that he has done.

Ever since I got the news I have been asking, why? Of course I have. The question keeps me awake every night as I lie there, raking over everything I can remember about Pamela's life with him. So I'm hoping for an answer as I enter his domain. All is in order. A filing system, neatly labelled, papers ordered. Everything I need comes easily to hand. He has made sure of that. They say the balance of his mind was disturbed, but there is no evidence of that here.

He was meticulous, a worrier, a taker of pains. He was always deliberate, never spontaneous. He planned it. I have no doubt of that. But why?

There are no answers here.

I have a last mission to fulfil. Their teacher suggested I send a memento to Josephine's friend, Susan, who moved away with her family earlier in the year. They were best friends, Miss Armstrong said, had kept on writing to each other. I remember her. She wasn't an obvious friend for Josephine: shy, quiet and not at all athletic. Doted on the dog, though. Rusty. Such a loyal friend. Poor old fellow. What an appalling last few minutes he must have had.

So, yes, Susan. Another only child, she was. Maybe that was the attraction. I'll probably find a shoebox in Pamela's wardrobe. I sidle sideways into the room to avoid looking at the blood-stained carpet. It will all be ripped up, but these things take time. There are all her shoes, stacked up in their boxes, the labels facing out. It takes over an hour. Because I end up looking at them all, wondering what to do with them. Clarks mostly. Nothing flashy, but always smart. Size 5 and a slender foot. In the end I just stack them up again and take the last pair out of their box. Hickory Glove Calf, it says on the label. So soft, and expensive, of course. 69/11. Over three pounds for a pair of shoes! But they're a classic court style so they would have lasted her. Would have.

There is something under the shoes, hidden by a sheet of tissue paper. A small volume of poems: W. B. Yeats, *Selected Poetry*. It falls open at 'When You Are Old'; such a well-known poem. Like most people, I suspect, I can recite the first two lines, find the whole first verse familiar, but have no idea what comes next. I read on and falter over the last lines, which are scored on either side by indentations. I can imagine Pamela running her thumbnail up and down, pressing into the paper. I read aloud:

> ...how Love fled
> And paced upon the mountains overhead
> And hid his face amid a crowd of stars.

I wander out of the room, clutching the book, my face streaming with tears. The phrase keeps repeating in my head. 'How Love fled...And hid his face...' I tuck the book carefully into my handbag. Then I blow my nose, wash my face at the kitchen sink and return upstairs.

I close the wardrobe door and move briskly to Josephine's room with the empty shoebox. What to put in it? I choose the book Josephine must have been reading. It's bookmarked, on her bedside table and she's written her name in the front. A book about a family. A family in a sailing boat. She must have loved it. I sit on the edge of the bed and read a few pages. So many times in the past I have sat here, reading aloud: Enid Blyton's *Mystery* series, and before that, *The Famous Five*. Then there was *The Children of the New Forest* – she loved anything involving danger and adventure.

Just like Pamela in that. Which is why, I slowly realise, that book of poetry is a surprise to me. Pamela never liked poetry. In fact she wasn't much of a reader at all. She was always out on her bicycle, or playing ball. Mad keen on getting into the netball team. And later on it was tennis. Forever practising her backhand against the garage wall. That little book is an enigma. Somewhere at the back of my mind I register that it might hold a secret, an answer to my question. But I'm not ready to explore that yet. And anyway, I haven't finished the task in hand.

I take another look around my granddaughter's bedroom. There's the postcard of the Empire State Building she was always so proud of. Harold said the view was magnificent from up there, but it gave me the heebie-jeebies to even think of being that high up. What an ordinary conversation that was. It seems to belong in another world. He could be so charming – I could see the attraction of the man right from the beginning. But I was never comfortable with him. He was – what's the word? Volatile. But Pamela steadied him. Should I have seen it coming? How could I? They were so devoted. He may have been volatile, but there was nothing to make you think… No. And anyway I wasn't here very often.

That poor child. Oh dear. It doesn't bear thinking of.

I sit down heavily on the bed and hold my head in my hands to stop them shaking. To think, here she was, sleeping. And then… If only I'd been here. But I doubt I could have saved them. A strange sound escapes my mouth. Like a yowling cat. This won't get me anywhere. I stand up too abruptly and have to steady myself on the desk as I walk to the window. I look down on the lawn where Pamela used to lay the tea table under the apple tree. The trouble is, what's the point? What's the point of me being here when they are not? I make myself turn away. I have a job to do.

On the desk is the red tartan pencil case Josephine always took to school. It's old and ink-stained but it will be familiar to her friend. I need something else to fill the box. My eye falls on Josephine's collection of dolls in national costume. That will be more cheerful. Maybe Susan has her own collection. Her father's in the Navy so he might bring them home from abroad. That one with the tambourine will do. Spanish, by the look of it. It's one of the more interesting ones. There. This afternoon I'll write a letter to go inside and parcel it up. Pamela always keeps brown paper and string in her bureau. When will I learn not to use the present tense?

In the lounge I get distracted, glaring at their possessions as if they can tell me something. I pick up a glass paperweight, remembering how I helped Josephine choose it for her father last Christmas. Oh, Josephine! No more outings to Liberty's. The pain is physical and so intense I have to sit down in the chair by the telephone. My gentle girl, so unassuming, so funny, such good company. I can't believe we'll never bake cakes together again or that you won't be helping me make jam.

I stare at their wedding photo. Pamela was a pretty bride. Pretty is the word for her. Not a beauty, but vivacious, the girl at the party everyone wanted to talk to. Friendly, attractive, not too intimidating. And him: brooding good looks was the best I could say. I remember meeting him for the first time.

'Mum, this is Harold!'

I turned from the sink and a shudder of something went through me. There was my Pamela with the sun catching her auburn hair and this man beside her with his arm round her shoulders, shutting out the light. Tall. Dark. Handsome. He was all of those. And Pamela, I could see, was radiant. So why the shudder? I felt betrayed. It was only a second.

Then I was wiping my hands on my apron, shaking hands, hugging Pamela, offering tea, calling Frank, taking them through. 'Where are your bags? Pamela, show Harold upstairs. I've put him in the green room. Tea will be ready directly.'

In bed that night I told Frank about my shudder.

'You just don't want anyone taking Pamela away,' he said.

'I never felt like that about that nice young doctor…'

'Ah, but he wasn't the one. It's clear this is the one she's set her heart on.'

'I suppose you're right,' I said. 'It was silliness, wasn't it?'

He squeezed my hand. 'Understandable silliness. I'll miss her too, you know.'

'He seems a nice enough young man, but…'

'He does.' Frank cut across my hesitation. 'A red-blooded chap with plenty of get-up-and-go. Obviously determined to get over this illness.'

'Yes, I suppose you're right.' I couldn't be wholehearted but

I couldn't pin down my reservation. It was true I didn't want anyone taking her from me and I resolved not to be a possessive mother. She was crazy about Harold. I'd never seen her look at a man the way she looked at him. An infatuation, I thought, and hoped it would pass. Then that nice Eric, the doctor, would pick up the pieces. But it didn't pass and she sent poor Eric packing.

'I'd hate to be a GP's wife,' she told me. 'Almost, but not quite, involved in the medical world. Anyway, I didn't love him.'

I suppose with hindsight you could say my reservation was a premonition. But I don't believe in that sort of thing. It wasn't that strong, anyway. Just a vague unease. I was perfectly prepared to welcome Harold into the family. He certainly set out to charm me – but never quite succeeded. He could be amusing, an asset at a party. But my vague unease grew into discomfort over the years. I worried about his moods and the way he laid down the law. Thank goodness Frank isn't here to see how completely he's taken her away from us. I couldn't have coped with his grief as well as my own. Being on my own, I can shut things out and get on with the practicalities. But if Frank were here, he'd know what I was up to and it would scupper me completely. That's what I tell myself, anyway.

It's a different story at two o'clock in the morning in my creaky bed at the top of the Royal Castle Hotel. The presence of Harold looms in from every corner of the crooked room like an ogre in a fairy tale. My obstinate mind insists on reimagining the family's last hour. Think of a flower. Think of a tree, the river, a sailing boat. But everything I determinedly picture leads me back to that garden, that house, that room, that man.

We couldn't have stopped her marrying him. I'm sure of that. Anything we said would have made her more determined. It might even have caused a rift, without achieving a thing. But I do blame myself for not seeing the signs. There must have been some, surely? She must have been unhappy. A thing like that doesn't happen out of a blue sky. Why didn't she confide in me? Did I pay too much attention to Josephine and not enough to Pamela? I liked to have Josephine stay with me, because then I didn't have to see Harold. I grimace into the darkness and beat my head on the pillow in shame at my selfishness. If only I'd gone to stay with them, I might have noticed. She might have said something.

I drift eventually into a half-waking, half-nightmaring state until the yakking and scrabbling of a herring gull outside the window rouses me. One sentence comes with me into the waking world. It beats its way into my brain as I brush my teeth and takes on Frank's tones as I roll on my stockings and fasten the suspenders: *Making him into a monster won't bring Pamela back*. Exactly the sort of thing Frank would have said. And true, of course. Frank used to say, 'He's a troubled soul. But Pamela can cope. She's got a handle on him.' Evidently not true.

Maybe she let go of that handle. I snap down the clasps of my suitcase on that thought and make my way to breakfast. Nasty hotel coffee and flabby toast. Smell of bacon and sausages turns my stomach. And where was I, her mother, when she needed me most? At home making green tomato chutney and listening to some band on the Light Programme. Totally oblivious. Having failed to notice anything. As I queue to pay my bill, Frank's voice comes again: *There's no earthly point blaming yourself. Where's that going to get you?*

On the train I finger the volume of poetry in my handbag. It was clearly very important to Pamela. And secret. Why else would you keep such a thing in a shoebox at the back of your wardrobe? I pull it out and flip through the pages looking for a scrap of paper, but none falls out. There is no inscription. Only those indentations provide the clue to the book's significance. I dare not read the poem in public in case it makes me cry again. Whatever it meant to her, the book – and Pamela – is being very discreet. I suddenly feel guilty of prying. The secret is her secret. Frank's voice tells me: *You can't live Pamela's life for her. She has to make her own mistakes.* It's something he reminded me of more than once over the years. No doubt he would also say that I couldn't have saved her from death either. It was her life, her death, her secret.

It's a relief to be home, away from that place. I unpack and undress and put all my clothes in the washing basket. I heat up a tin of tomato soup, but it doesn't warm me.

I make tea and sit in my chair where I feel safest. This has always been my reading chair, my knitting chair. It's a womb of a chair.

Frank's chair is still there on the opposite side of the fire. It's more upright, firmer, with wings like blinkers. Protective blinkers, they were. His was the chair that provided the milk money, the small change that fell from his pockets and which I scrabbled out from its short back and sides when the milkman called every Friday. I never resented the boundaries Frank set on our life together, but I did expand beyond them after he went.

I was cradled in my chair when the cat's waters broke on my lap, and later, when my own waters broke into its deep seat. I hold my mug of tea against my tummy, absorbing the heat.

It's as if I'm weighing my life in my hands. A gentleness creeps over me, an unexpected peace, gratitude that I am being allowed to live out my time. And maybe when it comes to its natural end I'll be sitting in this chair and it will once again soak up my bodily fluids. There will be no one to come and discover me. But that hardly matters. Probably the milkman will notice yesterday's pint still on the doorstep.

The house is cold, but it's not worth lighting a fire. I fill a hot water bottle and take it upstairs. Sleep comes quickly in my own bed.

In my dream a child comes running towards me in her nightie: fine lawn, a floral print, cool on summer nights. I remember stitching it. You are three years old, my lovely daughter, exuberant, trusting, your skin glowing from a bath, your hair a fiery halo.

As I stretch out my arms, you shapeshift and I'm looking into cooler eyes. You have become my granddaughter, Josephine, poised on a ledge above me.

I see earth beneath your pearly skin; roots for arteries; grass growing up behind the Liberty flowers.

When I wake up my pillow is damp. I lie there, as every morning when memory kicks in, rearranging the furniture of mind in line with what has taken place, and I take a shred of comfort from my dream.

Susan 2018

A letter came in the post today. A proper letter, not junk mail. Typed, but the envelope addressed in longhand. It was from the manager of the Cedars, a residential home in Dartmouth, informing me of the death of Miss Ursula Armstrong.

'I believe you may once have been one of her pupils. I thought you would want to know. Your name was among those she referred to frequently in the last weeks. We found your address on an old Christmas card. Miss Armstrong kept everything.'

Good heavens! It must be half a century since I saw Miss Armstrong, and the Christmas cards tailed off years ago. The letter went on to give details of the funeral.

'As someone who knew Miss Armstrong in her prime, perhaps you would care to say a few words…'

I don't think so. Why on earth would I attend the funeral of someone I've long lost touch with? Let alone "say a few words"? Definitely not.

But as I turn away, my eye rests on the photo Miss Armstrong sent me soon after Jo was murdered. There they are: Jo and Ginny and other "Hut" people with Miss Armstrong. It hangs above my desk among other group photographs from school and college days. I often wonder who took it. Probably one of the parents. Most likely Ginny's father, who loved to get involved and was often called upon to fix things – a broken door handle or a wobbly chair. It was unlikely to have been Mr Kennedy. He rarely came to the Hut, and I doubt Miss Armstrong would have asked him. Anyway, Jo wouldn't have been looking so relaxed and calm if her father had been behind the camera.

My only other mementoes of that time are the two old books that sit side by side on my bookshelf. Jo's Spanish doll ended up at the back of the wardrobe and, when I moved to this flat, it went to a jumble sale. Doesn't do to be sentimental.

The school logbook of the shipping activity on the river probably belongs in Dartmouth Museum, but I've always been oddly reluctant to let it go. I take it down and leaf through the pages. They are full of my handwriting and Jo's, complete with ink blots and spelling mistakes. It brings back powerful memories. By lunchtime I've bought a train ticket and booked myself into the Royal Castle Hotel.

What was it about Miss Armstrong that compels me to make this journey? On the train I have plenty of time to reflect upon that. I scribble the bullet points of my musings on the back of an envelope and allow myself to be prevailed upon to "say a few words".

'Miss Armstrong was no ordinary teacher,' I begin. 'She was enthusiastic about the Vikings and the Norse gods and only taught maths because she had to. I later discovered that she wasn't too accurate with the facts about her beloved Romans.' (A gentle titter from the sparse congregation.) 'But they were her true heroes and she inspired us with their values and culture. She taught us to love walking, the names of flowers and the flights of birds. We learned to respect the natural world, and she was a pioneer of ecology long before "Green" became a movement.' (A murmur of approval.) 'She was obstinate and opinionated, but she also listened. Above all, she taught us about trust and friendship and to look out for each other.'

To my horror, I hear my voice cracking. I take a deep breath.

'That is Ursula Armstrong as I remember her,' I conclude. When I return to my seat I find I am trembling. We struggle through "He Who Would Valiant Be", which for some reason conjures Miss Armstrong striding through the town, and finish with "Eternal Father Strong To Save", before we are released with the familiar exhortation, echoing down the years from my boarding-school, churchgoing days:

'Go forth into the world in peace; be of good courage; hold fast that which is good; render to no one evil for evil; strengthen the faint-hearted; support the weak; help the afflicted...'

Comforting phrases – not that I've ever lived up to them. I go in peace, but that which is good tends to elude me. In those days, you rendered evil to no *man*. Without that strong noun the sentence loses its punch. It's emasculated – which is the whole point, of course. As to the faint-hearted and the weak, I've never had much time for them.

I watch Miss Armstrong's little band of supporters from the Cedars make their unsteady way out of the church. It isn't entirely clear which are staff and which residents. I imagine following them back to the home to smile, bend and listen while juggling a cup of tea and a bun, and shudder inwardly. I make my excuses to the manager, and opt instead for a stiff drink in the hotel bar.

Next morning I order a taxi to Totnes and leave my suitcase in reception. I'm catching the afternoon train, so there's plenty of time to walk out to the castle and visit old haunts. At first glance, as I step onto the pavement, little has changed on the Quay.

I cross the road and look back to survey the scene. Cundell's has given way to Fat Face, but apart from that and the change in the size and shape of cars, it could be 1955. It feels surreal to be standing here, as if time has turned inside out. Dartmouth seems like a stage set. I half expect the shopfronts to shake as people go in and out, and the façade of the hotel to billow out in the draught of a door opening backstage.

But the buildings are as solid as they have been for hundreds of years. Yesterday, the dinghies marooned on the mud in the Boat Float looked shabby and neglected. This morning they appear workmanlike and seaworthy as they jostle and swing on the rising tide and raucous gulls strut about their decks. The pretence is all inside me. I have to admit, it is all about Jo – coming to the funeral, saying my piece. I was speaking of Miss Armstrong, but it was Jo I was there for. Fanciful as it appears to my logical brain, I was attending the ceremony in place of the ritual I missed sixty-odd years ago. And that last sentence, the one about friendship and trust that cracked my façade, that referred entirely to Jo. The friend I still miss.

I walk on, noticing that Lloyds Bank no longer occupies its familiar premises and that the Bay Tree in Fairfax Place is still an eating place, but now called Kendricks. The evening menu looks inviting. The Harbour Bookshop is no more – replaced by an art gallery with pictures for tourists. But the corner opposite hasn't changed. I cross over, following my plan to walk out to the castle. But as I reach the pavement where Jo and I stood all those years ago, eating our oranges, I find I cannot move. It's as if the spot is electrified, sending a current up through my legs. My body feels hot and immovably heavy on this bleak October day. I shake myself, try to shift my legs, but the effort required to put one foot in front of the other has me groping for the support of the low stone wall. This is ridiculous. I'm perfectly fit. I regularly walk a mile or two several times a week. Use it or lose it – that's my motto. I've seen plenty of people suffer because they did not take that simple precaution. I stand there clutching the wall and recognise that I cannot walk to the castle. But I have to get there. That was my plan and I have to complete it.

I turn slowly and cross the road. I'm aware of Pillar's the newsagent on my right. Shouldn't there be a hardware store straight ahead? Another damn art gallery. What's happened to this town? Indignation straightens me up. Head up. Shoulders back. I'm no frail old lady. I make my way down Hawley Road towards the river and happen on a kiosk where I can buy a ticket for the boat trip out to the castle. An obvious solution.

As soon as I start down the steps to board the ferry I regret it. There's no rail on the river side and the steps are wet and fringed with seaweed. Too late to turn back. The boatman takes one look at my teetering progress and bounds ashore to grab my hand. Normally I would pull away, but today I find his huge, calloused grip comforting.

'There we go, my lovely,' he says as he settles me into a corner seat.

I look around me and shudder. So much water. Jo was at home with it – it was her element, sailing, swimming, diving. Revisiting Dartmouth is turning into a pilgrimage. Heaven knows why, but I'm making this trip for Jo. What is that supposed to mean? It makes no logical sense.

I expect to wait for other passengers, but after a few minutes the boatman casts off. The jumping about and the play of ropes all looks very casual. I hope it's safe. But as the chug of the engine

145

accelerates, I find the throb of it beating up through the soles of my feet reassuring. It takes my mind off the fact that only a few planks of wood separate me from untold fathoms of water.

As we move into midstream I twist round to see what lies ahead. Waves slap against the hull and send up a spray that hits me sharply in the face. I shrink back, hurt and indignant, tasting salt, blinded by my own hair whipping my cheeks. Why the hell is there no cabin on this damn boat? I turn back and focus on the houses of Above Town with their steeply terraced gardens, gazebos and boathouses. Everything looks so much smarter than it did back in the fifties.

Warfleet Creek opens up with its dark wallow of green water and the Dartmouth Pottery building looming as a sinister backdrop. More fanciful thinking. It's just a grey stone edifice announcing WARFLEET in white lettering. But the creek itself does have an aura of magic, and not just because it was where Jo sailed and swam all summer. I wish we could turn in to its safe haven, away from the river currents and the wind off the sea, which is strengthening as we approach the mouth of the estuary.

But we've already left Warfleet behind and the boatman is pointing out a sculpture on the rocks at the water's edge. He tells a story about a mermaid staring wistfully out to sea. I'm not impressed, and he admits that the statue was only installed ten or twelve years ago. I thought as much. There were no wistful mermaids in my day.

Distracted by the story, I've failed to notice that, although we are close to the castle, the boat is heading out to sea. Where the hell is he taking me? The ferryman is just standing there, looking so relaxed with one hand on the tiller, but he must see the panic in my eyes as he looks up from his mobile phone.

Lazily, he pushes the wooden lever hard away from him, the boat swings round and he smiles back at me.

'No worries,' he says.

We head for Stumpy Steps. Although the manoeuvre is obviously standard practice, I feel as if I'm being teased and I'm indignant enough to ignore his offered hand as I step forward to disembark. But the sight of the water sloshing between the boat and the steps causes me to hesitate. He grips me by the hand and the elbow and virtually lifts me onto dry land. I inhale a mix of tarred rope and tobacco, and his body heat penetrates my coat. It is comforting. I thank him, feeling an overwhelming sense of gratitude.

'You're welcome,' he says, making it sound as if he really means it.

Wet steps give way to slithery leaves and mud as I climb up through the trees. It's steep, and I'm shocked to be out of breath when I reach the road. Tarmac at last. A car park and a café. Before heading in for a restorative coffee, I turn away towards the sea, lean on the wall and look down into Castle Cove.

There is blue sky overhead but the sea is still that headache-grey – a slatey swell cross-hatched by the wind, swirling green among rocks at the foot of the cliff and maintaining a steady simmer inside the cove directly below me.

But, as I look down, I'm seeing another day when the sea was quiet and the tide was out. I see myself and Ginny and Jo down there on the beach with a straight-backed Miss Armstrong, sitting among the rocks. Ginny is swigging from a lemonade bottle with her skirt ballooning in the wind, while Jo hands out the sandwiches. Bobby is in his swimming trunks, poking about in a rock pool that reflects blue sky and puffy clouds.

I shake away the image and look out across the gunmetal waves to the far horizon where a dark ridge has appeared. It advances steadily, dragging a cover over the blue. The roof is being closed on the sky – like on Centre Court at Wimbledon, but faster. The words of that Tennyson poem run through my head:

> *Break, break, break*
> *On thy cold gray stones, O sea!*

Break, break and keep on breaking over the stones, over the rocks and over the little group of precious people; breaking over the cliffs; breaking over the treetops.

As if the force of the inundation might sweep me away, I cling on to the wall to steady myself. A sudden shaft of sunlight pierces the cloud. The grey surface of the sea shatters into a million crystal shards skidding across the mouth of the estuary to the opposite shore and that other, less noticeable, castle on the Kingswear side. My heart thunders and leaps into smithereens as if to join those chips of light. I hear myself gasp and clutch at my throat.

What happened there? Clouds close over the sun. I finger the rough surface of the stone under my hands, surprised to find myself still standing in my ordinary coat and scarf. My body is heavy with the weight of the grey rocks, but my heart is still dancing with the sunlight on the water. I feel both sad and elated.

An odd balance. It feels like a gift, but I don't know what to make of it. Maybe, for once, I don't need to understand. I wipe away tears and check my watch. Plenty of time. Turning my back on the sea, I set off on the walk back into town and find I have a spring in my step.

Author's Afterword

This is a work of fiction. It is based on the facts of a tragic event that took place in Dartmouth in the early hours of 11 October 1955. Howard Koppenhagen, co-director of Dartmouth Pottery, murdered his wife, Patricia, twelve-year-old daughter, Christine, and Rusty, the dog. He then took his own life.

Why did he do this? This novella is an attempt to answer that question. I have chosen to work with fictional characters in order to distance the story from the real people involved. The sequence of events leading to the tragedy is wholly imaginary – so almost certainly not how it was in real life. In the same way, I never pursued a career in the police force, and – unlike Susan – am blessed with a wonderful husband.

Chris Koppenhagen was my friend. My intention is simply to pay tribute to Chris and her short life, and to explore how and why the tragedy came about. The aim is to lay ghosts to rest, rather than stir them up. I hope not to cause discomfort or distress to anyone who remembers this terrible event or to any descendant of those associated with the Koppenhagen family.

Lightning Source UK Ltd.
Milton Keynes UK
UKHW011953220519
343149UK00002B/76/P